D0049307

Match Wits with The Hardy Boys®!

Collect the Original
Hardy Boys Mystery Stories®
by Franklin W. Dixon

Celebrate 60 Years with the World's Greatest Super Sleuths!

The Great Airport Mystery

Valuable electronic parts containing platinum are being stolen from shipments made by Stanwide Mining Equipment Company's cargo planes, and Frank and Joe Hardy are called upon to assist their world-renowned detective father solve the baffling case.

At Stanwide the boys pose as employees, and become suspicious of their boss's hostility toward them. Is he involved in the racket? And what is the truth behind the plane crash at sea in which Clint Hill, chief pilot for Stanwide, was killed?

Frank and Joe launch an aerial search for clues to the platinum thieves' hideout, believing that they will also uncover the mystery behind Hill's accident. The puzzling trail of clues leads the young sleuths to an uninhabited Caribbean island, near the scene of the plane crash—then to a mountaintop in Montana and a danger-filled show-down with the band of thieves. But the final discovery—and most startling and exciting revelation of all—is made in the boys' home town of Bayport.

Franklin W. Dixon fans will find suspense, action, and many breath-taking flying episodes in this thrilling story.

"Those ropes will snap any minute!" Frank
thought fearfully

The Hardy Boys Mystery Stories®

THE GREAT AIRPORT MYSTERY

BY

FRANKLIN W. DIXON

GROSSET & DUNLAP
Publishers • New York
A member of The Putnam & Grosset Group

PRINTED ON RECYCLED PAPER

Copyright © 1965, 1957, 1930 by Simon & Schuster, Inc. All rights reserved.
Published by Grosset & Dunlap, Inc., a member of The Putnam &
Grosset Group, New York. Published simultaneously in Canada. Printed in the U.S.A.
THE HARDY BOYS® is a registered trademark of Simon & Schuster, Inc.
Library of Congress Catalog Card Number: 65-20038 ISBN 0-448-08909-2
1992 Printing

CONTENTS

CHAPTER I

Mysterious Flare

"Too bad we lost so much time fixing that flat, Joe. Dad wanted us home in a hurry to start work on a case."

Frank Hardy speeded up the brothers' convertible.

Joe studied a road map. "We're coming to a turnoff that could save us thirty miles," he said. "Let's try it."

The boys kept a sharp lookout in the gathering dusk. Presently Frank slowed and spun the wheel. The entrance to the turnoff was narrow and flanked by heavy trees and brush. If they had not been watching for it, they could easily have missed it.

A second later Frank slammed on the brakes. The glare of their headlights showed a wooden barrier several yards ahead.

"Oh, no! A roadblock!" Joe groaned.

"That's strange," Frank murmured. "There's no sign to explain why the road's cut off."

"Maybe it's only for minor repairs," Joe said hopefully. "Let's take a chance." He jumped out to move the wood barrier.

"Okay, but keep your fingers crossed," Frank said. "I'd sure hate to get stuck in some pothole and break an axle—especially at this time of night."

Joe, blond and a year younger than dark-haired, eighteen-year-old Frank, dragged the barrier aside. Frank drove past, then Joe replaced the roadblock to its original position.

Climbing into the convertible again, he asked, "Any idea what this new case Dad's working on is about?"

"No, but the way he sounded, it must be urgent."

Fenton Hardy, the boys' father, was a former crack detective of the New York City Police Department. After retiring from the force to the waterfront town of Bayport, he had become a famous private investigator.

Frank and Joe, who seemed to have inherited their father's sleuthing talents, often aided him in his investigations. The brothers had also solved several cases largely on their own, beginning with *The Tower Treasure*, and, most recently, the strange *Mystery of Cabin Island*.

Now a summer vacation trip had been cut short

by the upcoming assignment. The boys continued their journey in the deepening darkness. Ahead, the road wound through isolated, hilly country. Here and there they encountered patches of light radiation fog, a phenomenon common to this type of terrain. After several minutes the Hardys were puzzled not to see any road construction, or any other reason for the barrier they had encountered.

"Maybe the roadblock was just somebody's idea of a joke," said Joe.

Frank was about to answer when suddenly the brothers were startled to see an intensely bright red glow appear on the road ahead. Temporarily blinded by the light, Frank jammed on the brakes. The car skidded crazily, then came to a halt up on the side of a steep embankment that bordered the road.

"What's that?" Joe shouted.

"Looks like a flare!" Frank answered, turning off the ignition.

The boys' eyes became accustomed to the bright light just in time to spot a man scurrying off the road and into the woods. The stranger vanished quickly, but not fast enough to prevent the Hardys from getting a glimpse of his face. A split second later they heard a series of loud cracking sounds.

"Those are rifle shots!" Joe yelled. "But where are they coming from?"

"The woods. And they may be aimed at us! This

car is too good a target. We'd better get out pronto!"

But before either of the boys could move, a new sound captured their attention. The mounting, throaty drone was unmistakable.

"That's an airplane coming down!" Frank cried out.

"And it's headed this way!" Joe yelled.

At that moment the boys saw two bright lights approaching obliquely from the right and very low. Frank and Joe were able to make out its silhouette against the night sky, even through the glow of the flare. The plane had two engines and a sleek, streamlined fuselage that terminated at the rear in a high, swept-back tail section. Its landing gear was fully extended.

"That pilot's trying to set her down here!" Frank declared as he stared in disbelief.

"He's so low his wheels won't clear the top of our car! Get down!" Joe yelled frantically.

No sooner had the brothers dived to the floor of the car than the plane passed overhead with an earsplitting roar. Its left wheel grazed the roof of the car. Already tilted on the embankment, the convertible toppled over with a smash. The Hardys blacked out.

Several minutes passed before either of them regained consciousness. Frank was the first to move. With great effort he and Joe managed to push themselves to an upright position.

"Get down!" Joe yelled

"You all right?" Frank asked weakly.

"I feel as if I'd taken a ride inside a cement mixer." Joe groaned.

As their heads cleared, the brothers realized that the car was lying on its side. They forced open the door on Joe's side and scrambled onto the road, then glanced about them. The flare was gone, and the woods remained dark and silent. As far as they could tell, there was no sign of the airplane.

Frank bent down, and with his pocket flashlight, examined a deep crease across the roof of the overturned car. "It's from the wheel that turned us over," he commented.

"What was that idiot pilot doing?" Joe snapped.

"I don't know," Frank answered. "If he was trying to make a forced landing, he would have crashed into the trees on the other side of the road. Yet there's not a trace of any wreck."

"It vanished just like everything else," Joe said. "The flare, the man who ran into the woods as we drove up, and whoever was using the rifle."

"Did you get a look at the face of the man with the flare?" Frank queried.

"Yes, but only for an instant," Joe answered. "I think I've seen him some place before, though."

"Me, too," Frank agreed. "Maybe we saw a photo of him in Dad's files. Let's take a look when we get home."

Except for several deep dents and scratches, the

car did not appear to have suffered any serious damage. The boys decided to try rolling it back to an upright position.

"We'll need a couple of long poles for leverage," said Frank.

"Maybe we can find something in the woods," Joe suggested.

The boys took a flashlight from the car and started into the wooded area. They searched the ground carefully for fallen trees to serve as poles. Suddenly they were startled by a sharp, snapping sound, like the breaking of a twig, behind them.

"Did you hear that?" Joe whispered.

"Yes. Listen!"

There was a second snap. Then silence. The boys stared into the darkness, but could see nothing.

"Probably some animal," Frank said.

"I guess so," Joe agreed.

The Hardys were about to resume their search when the snapping of twigs was heard again. Frank switched off the flashlight. The boys listened. From nearby came the faint rustle of leaves. It was as if someone, or something, were approaching stealthily.

They turned and looked behind them. Suddenly the outline of a man appeared against the heavy brush. He seemed to be pointing something at them. Was he the man with the rifle? The Hardys stood frozen in their tracks.

CHAPTER II

Factory Detectives

"Who are you?" Frank demanded. He snapped on his flashlight and directed the beam toward the mysterious figure. He was not the man who had set the flare.

"Drop that light!" the stranger ordered gruffly.

Frank tossed the flashlight to the ground. The man then played a bright light of his own on the Hardys' faces and slowly stepped toward them. As he approached, the boys could see that he was armed with a double-barreled shotgun.

"What are you doing here?" he growled.

"Our car turned over," Frank began, "and we're looking for—"

"What's that you say?" the man shouted, cocking an ear toward Frank. "Speak louder!"

"I said our car turned over," Frank shouted, "and we are—"

8

"Your car turned over?" the stranger interrupted. "How did that happen?"

"The wheel of an airplane struck the roof."

"Airplane? What airplane? Speak louder!"

The stranger was apparently so hard of hearing he had not heard the noise. On the other hand, the boys wondered if he could be connected with the mysterious events that had occurred earlier and was bluffing. They decided to force the issue. Frank told him briefly about the roadblock, the red flare, and the low-flying plane. He also mentioned seeing a man run off the road into the woods, and said that later they had thought they were being shot at.

"You're both crazy," the stranger sneered. "I didn't see any airplane or red flare."

He then motioned with his flashlight for the boys to walk on past him. "You'd better get out of here right now, if you know what's good for you! You're on private property!"

"We didn't notice any fences or signs around here," Joe retorted.

"I don't care what you didn't notice!" the man shouted. "Get going!"

As the boys walked past him, they managed to catch a closer glimpse of his face. They saw that he was middle-aged, and pale and haggard.

Frank asked that he and Joe be allowed to find a couple of poles. The stranger hesitated, then gave permission.

Frank and Joe soon located several fallen saplings. They picked two of the strongest and dragged them to the car. They then positioned the saplings under the convertible and pushed against them with all their strength. At first it seemed hopeless, but after another powerful lunge, the car began to move, then shivered to an upright position.

The brothers stopped for a moment to catch their breath. They noticed that the stranger was watching them from the edge of the woods.

"Get going!" he yelled angrily.

Frank tugged at the jammed door on the driver's side. Finally it opened. The boys got in and Frank turned the ignition key. After a few seconds the engine came to life. Except for the draining off of some fuel and oil, the car seemed to be in safe-driving condition. Frank maneuvered it carefully for a few minutes, then gathered speed and set off for home.

"Wow!" Joe sighed. "I like excitement, but tonight was enough to last me for a month."

Trying to find some answers to all that had happened, the brothers discussed the mystery, but were unable to arrive at any conclusions. As they got closer to home, their thoughts shifted to the telephone call from their father. What could the case be? Their faces lit up in anticipation.

Nearly three hours later the boys reached Bayport, where they lived. As they entered the living room of the Hardy house, their mother greeted them. She was an attractive, slender woman, who tried to take the adventurous life of her family philosophically. Mrs. Hardy could not help worrying, however, over the dangers she knew they must encounter.

"Hello, sons," she said in a relieved voice.

"Hello, Mother," the boys answered, and Frank added, "Sorry to be so long driving back, but we took a short cut that turned out to be time consuming."

"My goodness, what happened to you two?" she asked in alarm as they bent down to kiss her. She pulled them closer to a lamp. Joe had a large swelling near his temple, Frank an ugly bruise under his left eye.

Mrs. Hardy wanted to call the doctor, but the boys assured her that their injuries were not serious. In order not to upset her further, Frank said they had been bruised when he had stopped the car short.

Miss Gertrude Hardy, sister of the boys' father, entered the room. She was a tall woman who secretly adored her nephews but constantly scolded them for not being cautious enough in their sleuthing. Occasionally her dire predictions of danger came true! At seeing their injuries, she immediately said, "Ice packs for both of you!"

"Please, Aunty, not until we talk to Dad," Frank pleaded.

The brothers hurried to their father's study. Mr. Hardy looked up as they entered.

"Hello, boys," he said. "Glad to see you back. Sorry I had to break up your visit." Noticing their injuries, he asked, "What happened?"

Joe told Mr. Hardy about their adventure while Frank began to hunt through the identification files. Several minutes later he held up a card.

"I found it!" he exclaimed. "Joe, I'm sure this is the man with the flare who ran into the woods!"

Joe looked at the photograph mounted on the card. "You're right!"

Frank handed the card to his father. Mr. Hardy took it and leaned back in his chair. He was a handsome, athletic-looking man.

"Ah, yes," he said. "I seem to remember this man. He's an ex-convict known only by the name of Bush Barney—no aliases. He served a three-year term for robbery."

"I wonder," said Joe, "if there's some connection between Bush Barney and that airplane we saw. Could the pilot have been dropping stolen merchandise to him?"

"It's a possibility," Frank replied. He reached for the telephone and began dialing a number. "I'm going to check with the control tower at Bayport Airport to see if they know of any aircraft that is overdue."

Frank identified himself to the tower operator

on duty, then questioned him. He was told that all flight plans to and from Bayport had been properly closed. The tower operator also said that transient aircraft, as well as those permanently based on the field, had been accounted for. Frank hung up, disappointed that he had not uncovered a lead.

Meanwhile, Mr. Hardy had been jotting down a few notes on Bush Barney. "Perhaps," he said, "the incidents you have told me may be linked to a new case I have coming up. That's why I asked you boys to come back."

Mr. Hardy stated that earlier in the day he had received a visit from a Mr. Albert Allen, president of the Stanwide Mining Equipment Company. The plant was located on the north edge of Bayport Airport, and manufactured mechanical and electronic tools and other equipment for the mining industry.

Mr. Allen had told the detective he was certain he had unearthed a racket within his company. He had been getting complaints from customers about shortages in orders. In each instance, a typed note had been enclosed in the shipment promising that the shortage would be made up at a later date. But the promise had never been kept, the customers said, and they needed the material.

"What sort of material have the shortages involved?" Frank asked.

"Mostly small, but expensive, components," his father answered. "Especially electronic parts with a high platinum content."

Mr. Allen, the detective continued, had ordered an examination of the company's books. Everything had tallied.

Recently he had had a meeting with a Mr. Cosgrove, whose firm was one of Stanwide's largest customers. Mr. Cosgrove had threatened to sever business relations with Stanwide because of the shortages. The publicity resulting from such a move could be extremely damaging to Stanwide, Mr. Hardy said—even more damaging than the loss in orders.

"It sounds like an interesting case," said Joe. "When do we begin?"

"Tomorrow," Mr. Hardy said. "First we're going to stop at the doctor's office and have him check those bruises of yours. Then we'll drive out to Stanwide to meet Mr. Allen. I'm arranging to have you boys pose as company employees."

"Employees?" queried Frank.

"Yes," his father answered. "Actually, you are going to be doing a factory investigation job."

CHAPTER III

The Ghost Pilot

THE next morning, after the doctor had assured Mr. Hardy that the boys were fit, the detective and his two sons proceeded to the Stanwide Mining Equipment Company for a meeting with Mr. Allen. Soon they were being ushered into a spacious, paneled office.

A graying, distinguished-looking man arose from behind a desk and extended his hand in greeting. Mr. Hardy introduced Frank and Joe. After handshakes Mr. Allen gestured for all of them to take chairs.

The tall executive studied the boys for a moment, then glanced at Mr. Hardy. "I've already made arrangements for your sons to be hired as summer employees of our firm."

"Good," Mr. Hardy answered. "I'm convinced that this is the only way the case will be solved—by someone working on the inside."

"Our posing as employees," Frank spoke up, "will allow Joe and me to investigate without anyone becoming suspicious."

"I hate to think that any of my employees may be mixed up in this," Mr. Allen said with a sigh. "However, I'll do anything to help clear up the mystery."

"Dad tells us that most of the shortages are of parts that contain platinum," Joe remarked.

"That's correct," replied Mr. Allen. "It's understandable, too, for they would be the most valuable."

"Where do you obtain your platinum?" Frank queried.

"We purchase it in large quantities from a firm in Canada."

As they discussed the case, Mr. Allen noticed the brothers glancing at a strange voodoo figurine mounted on the wall.

"I see you boys are interested in my little curio," he said.

"Yes, we are," Frank admitted.

"The figurine is more to me than just an ornament," Mr. Allen said sadly. "It is also a reminder of a tragedy that occurred several months ago."

The Hardys listened intently as he related the story. His firm owned a subsidiary company known as Stanwide Research and Development Laboratories. Its function was to conduct exploratory mining work in various parts of the world.

Recently, an expedition had been sent in one of the firm's aircraft to Ile de la Mer, a small uninhabited island far out in the Caribbean. During the return trip the plane had developed engine trouble and crashed into the sea. Only the copilot, Lance Peterson, had survived. The pilot, Clint Hill, and three mineralogists had gone down in the sinking aircraft. Lance Peterson was now chief pilot for the company.

"I considered Clint Hill not only a loyal employee," said Mr. Allen, "but also a close friend. It was Clint who sent me the figurine. I was shocked and grieved when he was lost."

Mr. Allen sat silent for a few seconds, then came back to the case at hand.

"Now, about your employment," he said to the boys. "Your father asked me to select jobs that would give you as much freedom to roam around the plant as possible. I think an assignment as plant messengers would fill the bill."

"That's perfect," Mr. Hardy agreed.

Mr. Allen asked the boys when they would like to start.

"How about tomorrow?" Frank suggested. "The sooner the better."

Mr. Hardy informed his sons that right now he and Mr. Allen were going to examine the firm's employee files for possible suspects. He suggested that in the meantime Frank and Joe become acquainted with the layout of the plant.

Mr. Allen had one of his office clerks take the young detectives on a brief tour of Stanwide. Then they were introduced to Art Rodax, the man who was to be their boss. Rodax was heavy-set, with thinning hair and a sour-faced, belligerent expression. He seemed to develop an immediate dislike for the two new employees.

"Factory messengers, eh?" he blurted. "I don't need any more help."

"But we've already been hired," said Joe. "We start tomorrow morning."

"Then I guess there's nothing I can do about it," Rodax growled. "But let me catch you lying down on the job just once and you won't last a day."

He was still grumbling when the boys left to return to Mr. Allen's office.

"Boy!" Joe exploded. "I'm sure glad we aren't really going to be working for that sourball."

"Me too," said Frank. "He'd make a starving man lose his appetite!"

Mr. Hardy told the boys that his examination of the employee files would take longer than expected. Since Mr. Allen had offered to drive him home later, he suggested that his sons take the car and go now.

"When I get home I'll let you know if I find out anything," the detective promised.

"Okay, Dad," said Frank. "Joe and I want to

stop at the airport on the way back to double-check with Lou at the tower on all of last night's flights."

Light rain was falling, and a heavy prefrontal fog was beginning to move in as the Hardys arrived at the field. They walked to the tower and climbed the winding steps to the top.

As they entered the control room, Lou Diamond, the tower chief, waved a greeting. A short, stocky, good-natured man, with crew-cut red hair, he nevertheless had an air of authority.

"You boys picked a fine day to pay us a visit," he said with a laugh. "In a little while that fog will be so thick you can walk on it."

The Hardys peered through the tinted panes of glass enclosing the control room. Already the ramp area immediately below was vanishing in a milky fog.

"We're not here just for a visit," Frank announced. "We thought you might help us by giving out some information."

The young detectives then told the tower chief about their encounter with the low-flying aircraft the night before.

"Were you able to identify the type of aircraft, or get its registration number?" Diamond asked.

"It was too dark for positive identification," Joe replied. "Anyway, we were both busy ducking!"

Diamond looked thoughtful. "Funny. I know of

no private landing fields in that area." He paused. "There have been several strange things going on in the air around here lately," he said.

"What kind of strange things?" Frank asked.

"At night we've picked up messages between planes that must be in code. They sure make no sense."

Suddenly a light flashed on the console and one of the radio speakers crackled to life. It was the unicom frequency used by flight students for practice and by pilots wishing to communicate with one another in the air.

"Bayport tower! This is Highflite One-Four-Alfa!" the pilot identified his craft, using Alfa for A. "How do you read?"

To the boys' astonishment, the tower chief's normally ruddy face turned pale. He picked up a microphone, then stood motionless, apparently unable to speak. Finally, in a quivering voice, he responded:

"High . . . Highflite One-Four-Alfa! This is Bayport tower. Reading you loud and clear."

"This is One-Four-Alfa. Not on an instrument flight plan. We are on top at thirteen thousand. Can you get us cleared for an ILS approach at Bayport?"

"Negative, One-Four-Alfa," replied the tower chief. "Bayport is now below ILS minimums. Advise you contact Air Traffic Control on the proper frequency."

There was no answer from the aircraft. Diamond seemed to be under a great strain. He placed the microphone on a table and mopped perspiration from his face.

"What's wrong?" Frank asked anxiously.

"The aircraft that just called! That identification number!" the tower chief said in a shaky voice.

"What about the identification?" Joe urged.

"That's the number of the plane once owned by Stanwide Mining! The one that crashed in the sea several months ago!"

"M-m-m, that surely is strange," Frank said, frowning.

"I don't know what's going on," replied the tower chief. "But I'm sure of one thing. The pilot who called sounded exactly like Clint Hill!"

Just then the radio speaker again crackled to life. A weird sound, like a disembodied chuckle, came eerily from it. Then a voice spoke. "The dead can tell no tales!"

"That *is* Clint Hill!" Diamond murmured, looking like a ghost himself.

"What do you make of it?" Frank asked.

"Only one thing," said Diamond in a frightened voice. "I never used to believe in ghosts. But now I do!"

CHAPTER IV

Police Orders

FRANK and Joe, startled by the unearthly voice, were equally amazed by the tower chief's admission that he believed in ghosts!

"There must be some other explanation," Frank said.

"Well, maybe. I guess I lost my head for a moment. But there's no way we can check on the aircraft," Diamond declared. "Our field doesn't have airport surveillance radar, and the pilot said he wasn't on an instrument flight plan, so Air Traffic Control wouldn't have any record on him."

"You are required to keep a record on tape of all two-way communications between the tower and aircraft, aren't you?" asked Frank.

"Yes," Diamond replied.

"Could it be arranged for us to borrow a copy of the tape with Hill's voice on it?"

"I'll have to check with our regional office," said the tower chief. "But in view of the circumstances, I'm sure it will be all right."

The boys, puzzled by this airport mystery, left the control tower and headed for the terminal building.

"Let's find a telephone and call Mr. Allen," said Frank. "I want to tell him what happened, and also ask him where we can find Lance Peterson."

Mr. Allen was astounded at hearing the news about Clint Hill. He was certain that it was someone's gruesome idea of a joke. Frank then asked him if he had heard anything about the strange coded messages that Lou Diamond had mentioned.

"No, I haven't."

Frank next inquired where he could find Lance Peterson, and was told that he should be in his office at the Stanwide hangar.

The Hardys walked along the north side of the Bayport field until they came to the Stanwide hangar. It was a huge metal and stone structure with a high convex roof. On each side of the building were lean-tos which housed the shops and offices of the company's flight operations. The door to one of these offices was marked CHIEF PILOT.

The Hardys knocked, then opened the door and walked in. Standing near a window was a man of average height, with sandy-colored hair and a hard, weathered face. He turned and stared at the Hardys as they entered.

"Mr. Peterson?" asked Frank.

"That's right," the man replied. "What can I do for you?"

The boys introduced themselves and announced that they would like to ask him a few questions. Peterson agreed, and appeared quite calm and pleasant until Frank asked him about the crash at sea in which Clint Hill had been lost. Peterson's face paled. He nervously sat down behind his desk and clutched both sides of the chair.

"We crashed, and that's all there is to it!" he snapped. "Let's drop the subject."

"What was the cause of the crash?" Joe asked.

"The airplane's at the bottom of the ocean," said the pilot. "There's no way I can check for the reasons."

"You were in the plane," Frank countered. "Can't you make a guess?"

"Both engines quit," Peterson said. "In those circumstances, fuel contamination is the most probable cause."

"Are you certain Clint Hill is dead?" Joe queried.

"Of course he is!" Peterson answered impatiently. "Why do you ask that?"

"Because his ghost contacted the tower just a little while ago," Frank announced.

"I'm not in the mood for bad jokes," shouted the pilot, leaping to his feet. He glanced at his wrist watch. "Anyway, I'm scheduled to fly in a few minutes. I'll have to go."

The boys left the office, with Peterson trailing close behind them. He pulled the door shut, locked it, then walked off without saying another word.

"What do you make of him?" Joe asked his brother.

"Our questions sure made him uneasy. If you ask me, he's trying to cover up something."

The young detectives decided to look around the hangar for possible clues to the mystery. They entered by a side door and acted very casual, as if interested only in seeing the aircraft stored there. They had covered nearly half the premises when a young man came strolling out of the pilots' lounge.

"Hey, look!" said Joe. "There's Jerry Madden!"

The young pilot was a wiry, good-looking youth whose brother was a teammate of the Hardys on the school's varsity football squad.

"Hello, Jerry!" called Frank.

Jerry turned. When he saw the boys, who ran to meet him, his face broke into a wide smile.

"Hi! What are you fellows doing out here at our lil ole aerodrome?" he asked with a laugh. "Getting the yen to do some aviating?"

"We'd like nothing better than a short hop in a sightseeing plane," Frank said with a grin, in an effort to explain their presence without arousing Jerry's curiosity. "But the weather has other ideas. So we decided just to roam around and look at the planes."

"What are *you* doing here?" Joe asked Jerry.

"I have a job flying for the Stanwide company," Jerry explained. "I was hired soon after I received my instruments and multiengine ratings last spring."

As they talked, the boys were not aware that a uniformed policeman was approaching from behind. The officer hailed them.

"What are you fellows doing here?" he demanded.

"I work here, Officer," Jerry said.

"And who are you two?" the policeman said, eying the Hardys carefully.

"They're Frank and—" Jerry began.

"Let them speak for themselves," interrupted the policeman.

"I'm Frank Hardy. This is my brother, Joe. We're going to work for Stanwide."

"I'll have to see some identification."

The boys extracted cards from their wallets and handed them to the policeman. He examined the cards, then suddenly became apologetic.

"I know of you and your father by reputation," he said. "Sorry to have bothered you."

Suddenly Joe sensed that they were being watched. He glanced to his left, without turning his head, and out of the corner of his eye glimpsed a man's face peering at them from behind an airplane near the entrance. But the face drew back out of sight before Joe could distinguish the features.

"Are you boys here on a case?" the policeman asked.

"We're on vacation. This is a summer job," Joe replied, speaking more loudly than usual for the benefit of the man behind the plane. "We were just looking at the company's airplanes." He nudged Frank to agree.

"What seems to be the trouble, Officer?" Jerry questioned.

"Our desk sergeant received a call saying that two prowlers had been seen in this hangar," the policeman explained.

"Do you know who made the call?" Frank asked.

"No, it was anonymous."

Joe glanced in the direction where he had seen the face. It did not reappear. He motioned Frank to keep talking, then darted to where he had spotted the eavesdropper. No one was there.

The young detective quietly moved in the direction he thought the stranger must have taken. Joe found it awkward trying to maneuver, unseen, around the closely packed aircraft. Suddenly he spotted a stocky man in mechanic's clothes walking quickly toward Lance Peterson's office. Joe hid behind the tail section of an aircraft and watched. Upon reaching Peterson's door, the mechanic anxiously jiggled the knob. Finding it locked, he walked away and out of sight.

Joe returned to Frank and the others. He apologized for going off so abruptly. "Thought I saw one of the real prowlers, but I must have been mistaken."

"How many mechanics do you have working here, Jerry?" Frank asked.

"Eight," he answered. "But there's only one on duty in the hangar today—Mike Zimm. Why do you ask?"

"Oh, I'm just curious," Frank said nonchalantly. "Joe, it's time we started for home."

The boys, accompanied by Jerry and the policeman, walked toward the door of the hangar. As they neared it, Frank and Joe noticed something that brought them to a stop. On the floor lay a splintered section of wooden board.

The boys thought it strange that a piece of debris like that should be left on a floor so spotlessly clean.

Apparently the policeman thought so too. He bent down and picked up the board. Under it was a set of footprints, embedded deeply in the concrete.

"I wonder whose they are," said Frank.

Jerry Madden moved closer and gazed down at the floor.

"I know whose footprints they are," he said. "Clint Hill's."

CHAPTER V

Warehouse Crash

"CLINT Hill's footprints!" Joe exclaimed. "How do you know, Jerry?"

"The head of our company, Mr. Allen, was very fond of Clint," the pilot explained. "Shortly before he was lost in a crash at sea, the hangar floor was resurfaced with new concrete. Mr. Allen, perhaps partly in fun, asked Clint to make the prints. I wasn't here at the time, but it's a well-known story around the flight department."

The Hardys studied the footprints carefully. They noticed that the instep of the right foot was narrower than that of the left.

The policeman, who had to get back to his regular duties, said good-by. Jerry watched his young detective friends as they continued their study of the prints.

"I saw something just before I met you fellows that perhaps I should tell you," he said.

30

"What's that?" Frank asked.

"A man's arm reached in through the door and placed that board over the prints," Jerry explained.

"That's funny," Frank commented.

Jerry went on, "I didn't attach any importance to it at the time. In fact, I'd forgotten about it until I saw how interested you were in those prints. Maybe the person is still around."

The boys dashed outside the hangar, but saw no one.

"We've heard of Clint Hill a couple of times today," Joe told Jerry, but did not explain further.

After requesting Jerry to keep his eyes open and report to the Hardys any unusual goings-on around the hangar, the brothers left for home. Both were quiet, pondering over all that had happened during their visit to the hangar. Why had Hill's footprints been covered? Was it to make certain the boys would not see them? And who had reported the presence of two prowlers to the police? Then there was the mechanic, Mike Zimm. Had he been the man who had eavesdropped on their conversation? The case, the boys agreed, was becoming even more puzzling.

During supper they related their day's adventure to the family.

"Mighty queer business," Aunt Gertrude commented. "You boys had better watch your step. I don't know what we're coming to when a company's employees can't walk around its private hangar without someone setting the police on them!"

The boys and their parents smiled. They were used to Aunt Gertrude's outbursts. Frank and Joe assured her they would try to duck any danger.

The next morning, Thursday, the boys rose for an early breakfast, eager to start their work at the Stanwide factory. Dressed in light khaki work pants and shirts, and equipped with appetizing lunches prepared by their mother and Aunt Gertrude, they drove off to the plant.

Frank and Joe reported to their boss, Art Rodax, exactly on time. Apparently this was not good enough.

"I want all new workers in my department to be here twenty minutes early!" Rodax growled.

"Is that a company rule?" Joe asked in surprise.

"It's my rule!" Rodax announced angrily. "Break it just once and you're out!"

He then thrust two large handfuls of work orders at Frank and Joe.

"You've got thirty minutes to deliver these and get back here!" he bellowed.

The boys moved quickly and just managed to return on time. Rodax appeared to be disappointed. He had underestimated the Hardys' efficiency. To make their task harder, he gave them a number of other chores in addition to their regular duties.

That evening the brothers went to bed immediately after supper, completely exhausted. Their second day on the job did not differ much from the first. Frank and Joe noticed that other employees of the department were given little to do.

"Good thing the weekend's coming up," Joe grumbled. "The way Rodax drives us, he could have had all the Cape Kennedy gantries finished in two weeks!"

"What bothers me most," Frank complained, "is that we're not getting much of an opportunity to investigate."

Yet the boys did not want to report the situation to Mr. Allen. There would be little the executive could do to help, they thought, without arousing suspicion.

Monday the young detectives had an unexpected change in luck. Rodax was assigned for the day to another section of the factory to help supervise the installation of a new duplicating machine. Grateful to have comparative freedom, even if just for the short time, the boys divided the work orders assigned them.

"Meet me in the warehouse at lunch hour," said Frank. "We can compare notes then, and at the same time look around the building."

"See you there about twelve o'clock," Joe answered as he picked up a bundle of the orders and started off on his rounds.

Both boys watched carefully for anything suspicious in each department they visited. Not a single clue was uncovered to the mystery of the disappearance of Stanwide's platinum components.

A few minutes past noon Frank and Joe greeted each other in the firm's large warehouse. It was divided into two main sections for incoming and outgoing shipments. Stacks of cardboard boxes and wooden crates towered almost to the ceiling. There were also several pieces of heavy machinery stored along one wall in a neat row.

The Hardys found a wooden crate and sat down side by side to eat their lunches. They glanced around to make sure there were no other workers about. The only sound was the steady hum of the warehouse's ventilating system. As a precaution, the boys spoke in low voices.

"Did you have any luck?" Frank queried.

"I didn't come up with a single clue." Joe sighed with disappointment.

"I didn't find anything, either," Frank confessed.

He told Joe he had investigated the handling of shipments from beginning to end, even to checking the bills of lading to see if they had been tampered with. His examination had revealed nothing.

"Whoever's running this platinum racket is a slick operator," Joe remarked.

Unheard by the boys over the hum of the ventilating system, an overhead hoist was being put into operation. It was only a short distance behind the two young detectives. A heavy piece of machinery was slowly lifted off the floor, then edged to a position directly above Frank and Joe.

Suddenly the boys were startled to hear the sharp, metallic snap of a release clutch. This was immediately followed by a deep whirling sound directly above them. Frank and Joe looked up instantly. A massive bulk of metal was plunging toward them!

The boys made a frantic leap and went tumbling across the floor. The hurtling object pulverized the crate on which they had been seated, and sent splinters of wood and metal in all directions.

"That was close!" Joe exclaimed.

Frank said grimly, "Someone did that on purpose!"

As the boys scrambled to their feet, a door slammed violently at the far end of the warehouse. The Hardys ran to the door and flung it open. No one was in sight. They hurried outside and were about to search the area when they were confronted by a company guard.

"Hold it!" he ordered. "What's going on here?"

"Did you see anyone run from the warehouse just now?" asked Frank.

"No one but you two!" the guard retorted. "I thought I heard a loud crash inside the building. What happened?"

The boys told him of the incident, and added that immediately after the crash they had heard someone fleeing from the building.

The guard eyed them with suspicion. "We'd better go inside and take a look."

Frank and Joe were annoyed at being delayed but had no choice in the matter. The man herded them into the warehouse and peered down at the huge, twisted piece of machinery on the floor. It not only had crushed the wooden crate, but had embedded itself deep in the concrete floor.

"What's the big idea of lying about this?" he thundered. "You caused this accident, but you're blaming it on someone else!"

"We had nothing to do with it!" Joe protested angrily. "And besides, we might have been killed. We were sitting on that very crate."

"Oh, yeah?" the guard sneered.

Frank looked hard at the man. "We demand to see Mr. Allen!" he said.

"The head of the company?" the guard asked. "Fine chance of that. Mr. Allen's a busy man. He wouldn't have time to talk to a couple of kids."

"I wouldn't be too sure of that!" Joe warned.

The massive bulk of metal plunged toward the boys

The guard was bewildered by the demand. He broke into a nervous grin.

"We don't have to bother Mr. Allen," he said. "Somebody might lose his job because of this. Besides, this equipment is being discarded. Let's just forget the whole thing."

The young detectives did not answer. They left the warehouse and returned to their jobs.

"That guard certainly changed his attitude in a hurry when we asked to see Mr. Allen," Joe remarked.

"Perhaps he's afraid that he'd lose his own job for not keeping a closer eye on things," Frank suggested. "After what happened, we'd better watch our step around here!"

After supper that evening Frank and Joe joined their father in his study. The boys told him about their narrow escape, and of their failure to uncover any clues.

"I'm sure our real reason for working at Stanwide is suspected," said Frank.

Mr. Hardy agreed, and added, "As long as you continue to work at Stanwide, the thieves will probably lie low and you won't learn anything. Besides, it's too dangerous for you there. Your close call in the warehouse sounds as if the thieves are already trying desperately to get rid of you."

The sleuth advised his sons to report to Mr. Allen everything that had happened, then resign their jobs.

"Work on the case from the outside," he advised. "I'll arrange to obtain a clearance for you at the airport, so you can roam around just like the regular personnel."

Frank smiled. "Then we'll have lots of time to keep a close watch on Stanwide's hangar."

Joe nodded. "And also, I'd like to investigate the wooded area where we saw Bush Barney. That mystery hasn't been solved."

"Good idea," Frank replied. "And let's make our first look an over-all one—from the air."

CHAPTER VI

Aerial Mission

"THE meterologist at the airport says it should be clear tomorrow," Frank announced as he put down the telephone.

"I'll call Ace Air Service first thing in the morning and arrange to schedule an airplane," said Mr. Hardy. "What time do you boys want to take off?"

"We plan to photograph the wooded area with our aerial camera," Frank answered. "If we arrive there shortly after twelve o'clock, the sun will be almost directly overhead. There won't be any shadows from trees and other objects."

"Good thinking," Mr. Hardy said approvingly. "You'll be less likely to miss important details that might be hidden if there were shadows."

The investigator said that, meanwhile, he would check into the ownership of the land.

"If it *is* private property," said Joe, "I doubt it belongs to that fellow who chased us."

At that instant Aunt Gertrude entered the study, carrying a large tray of brownies and lemonade. She placed it on Mr. Hardy's desk.

"I'm sure you can all forget about your new case long enough to have a snack," she said in a cajoling voice.

"Frank and I have to watch what we eat," Joe said jokingly. "We don't want to get airsick tomorrow."

"Airsick?" the tall woman exclaimed, her eyes opening wider. "My word! So you boys intend to go flying around in a bouncy plane?"

"We're just going up to take some pictures of crooks," said Frank, grinning.

"Isn't your detective work dangerous enough here on the ground?" Aunt Gertrude asked sharply.

Mr. Hardy reached out and patted his sister on the shoulder. "Doing detective work while flying isn't any more of a risk than it is while riding in a car," he told her reassuringly.

But Miss Hardy was not convinced. "At least in an automobile"—she sighed—"you can get out and walk if the motor stops!" Shaking her head, she left the study.

"By the way," said Mr. Hardy, "a fellow from the Bayport control tower delivered a small package for you boys this morning."

He extracted a set of keys from his pocket, unlocked his desk drawer, and took out the package. Frank eagerly opened it while Joe went to fetch their tape recorder.

"This," Frank explained, "is the tape containing the conversation between the control tower and someone who sounds like Clint Hill. I thought if we listened to the recording several times, we might be able to identify the 'ghost' with one of our suspects."

At that moment a stout, cheerful-looking boy strolled into the study.

"Hi, Chet!" The Hardys grinned at the new arrival.

Good-natured Chet Morton was one of Frank and Joe's best pals. Although comfort-loving and not fond of danger, he was loyal and had often helped the brothers in solving mysteries.

"Hi, everyone!" Chet responded. Spotting the tray of refreshments, he eyed them hungrily.

"You're just in time for a little snack," said Frank, chuckling. Their friend's large appetite was well known to all!

"Thanks. I thought I'd stop by and see what you and Joe are up to!"

Just then Joe returned with the recorder. Frank put the tape on the machine and snapped the "Start" switch. Seconds later a ghostly voice issued from the speaker.

"What is that?" queried Chet with a look of genuine astonishment.

"You're listening to a ghost." Joe grinned.

"Ghost!" Chet replied scornfully. "That cater-wauling wouldn't even scare a nervous cat."

They played the tape several times. Chet tried to imitate the eerie voice.

"The dead can tell no tales!" said the tape.

"The dead can tell no tales!" Chet repeated.

"That's a pretty good imitation." Frank laughed. "Maybe you can get work haunting houses."

The Hardys listened to the tape a few more times, but were unable to associate the "ghost" with any of the suspects they had encountered.

Chet, who by now had consumed most of the brownies, glanced at his watch and announced it was time for him to go home. As he left the study, the boys were amused to hear him mumbling, "The dead can tell no tales!"

The next morning Frank and Joe drove to the Stanwide Mining Equipment Company. Mr. Allen welcomed them with a smile as they entered his office.

"How has the case been coming?" he asked. "Have you managed to uncover any clues?"

"We haven't found much to go on," Frank said regretfully.

The boys told him about their visit to the Stanwide hangar, and described all that had happened during their masquerade as employees. Mr. Allen expressed deep concern over their narrow escape in the warehouse.

The Hardys said they were certain that, somehow, information had leaked out as to their real reasons for working in the plant. He agreed that it might be too dangerous for them to continue their undercover work there.

"I'm disturbed to hear about Art Rodax's conduct," Mr. Allen declared. "I won't have a man of his character working for my company!"

"I suggest you say nothing to him," Frank urged. "Every one of your employees is a suspect at present. If Rodax is fired, it may spoil our chances of getting to the bottom of the platinum thefts."

Frank also pointed out that it would be unwise for Joe and himself to resign suddenly from their jobs. This might make it appear that their investigation had uncovered some clues and would put whoever was involved in the thefts doubly on guard.

"Then what will you do?" Mr. Allen asked.

"We'll get ourselves fired," said Frank.

"How?" his brother questioned.

"From the beginning, Rodax has resented our being hired," Frank said. "Maybe it's because he's mixed up in the racket, and he knows about us. Anyhow, I'm willing to bet he wouldn't need much of an excuse to fire us."

Frank glanced at his wrist watch. "You know how fussy he is about having us report for work twenty minutes early. Well, we're now nearly an hour late. That should do it."

After telling Mr. Allen that they would keep him posted on any new developments in the case, the young detectives went off to the messenger department. When they came face to face with Rodax, Frank could see that his plan was working out even better than he had expected.

"Do you know what time it is!" shouted Rodax. Although he seemed furious, the boys could sense that he was actually pleased with the situation.

"We couldn't get here any earlier," said Joe.

"You won't have to worry about that any more!" Rodax bellowed. "You're fired!"

The boys pretended to be angry and concerned. "We'll report this to the main office!" Frank blazed.

"Go ahead!" Rodax yelled. "See how far that will get you!" He turned and stalked off with a self-satisfied air.

The boys left the factory and started for the airfield. On the way they discussed Rodax briefly.

"I wonder how pleased old sour face would be," Joe remarked, "if he realized he'd played right into our hands!"

A few minutes later the Hardys were walking toward a small frame building. A sign reading

"Ace Air Service" spanned its entire width along the roof. Another, smaller sign, "Office & Operations," hung above the doorway. On the aircraft parking ramp the boys saw three single-engine and two multiengine aircraft bearing the firm's name. As they entered the building, a voice called to them:

"Frank and Joe Hardy?"

The boys turned to see a tall, lean man walking toward them. He wore a tan cloth jacket and sunglasses with green-tinted lenses. He extended his hand in greeting.

"I'm Randy Watson," he said. "I fly for Ace Air Service. I have a plane all set." The pilot added he had often flown their father on trips. "I've heard a lot about you fellows," he added, smiling. "Are you on a case, or just going on a sightseeing ride?"

Before answering, Frank walked over to a large aeronautical chart attached to the wall. With his finger he circled an area, colored in shades of light green and brown, northwest of Bayport.

"We want to take some aerial photographs in this locale," he said. "Joe and I are sure we spotted an ex-convict there. We're curious to know what he's up to."

Randy stepped close to the chart and estimated the distance between Bayport and the area Frank had indicated.

"That's not far by air," he observed. "We can use one of the single-engine ships."

"We'd like to reach the area about noon," said Frank.

The pilot checked his wrist watch. "That means we'll have to take off within the next ten or fifteen minutes."

Joe hurried to the airport restaurant to order sandwiches and milk for their lunch, while Frank returned to the brothers' car to pick up the aerial camera and films. The boys reached the flight line just as Randy was completing a preflight check of the aircraft. In a few minutes they were strapped in their seats and taxiing toward the active runway.

The pilot remarked, "Because of the direction of the wind, that runway is the only one I can use to head the plane into the wind."

He tuned his radio to the proper frequency and contacted Bayport tower. An immediate reply crackled from the plane's receiver.

"Ace Service Flight Two-Six is cleared to runway One-Niner. Wind's from the southeast at fifteen knots. Altimeter setting, Two-Niner-Eight-Six."

Randy paused to check his instruments, controls, and engine magnetos. The tower then cleared him for immediate take-off. Turning into the runway, he eased the throttle ahead. Soon he and his passengers were airborne and taking a course to the northwest.

The boys gazed down at the earth below. The terrain became more hilly with each passing mile. The expanses of wooded areas looked like rumpled deep-green carpet. Here and there, lakes and small streams reflected the sun in bright flashes almost blinding in their intensity.

The pilot adjusted his course, checked his watch against the small clock mounted on the instrument panel, then said to Frank and Joe, "We should be coming up on the area you're looking for in a few minutes."

The Hardys scanned the surface below more intently. Far to the left, Frank saw a narrow ribbon of paved road that he surmised to be the highway from which he and Joe had turned onto the secondary road. Frank requested the pilot to fly closer to the highway.

"There it is!" declared Joe. "That must be the secondary road we drove along!"

Frank peered directly downward. The road itself was not visible, but a telltale cleft that snaked among the trees told him it was there. Randy banked steeply to the right and paralleled the road.

"Can we fly lower?" Frank asked.

Randy examined the terrain. "It seems to be pretty desolate. I think we can drop to a lower altitude without breaking any air regulations."

The pilot eased back on the power and allowed the nose of the airplane to drop a few degrees below the horizon. The large hand of the altimeter slowly moved counterclockwise, indicating a descent.

Randy leveled out at about five hundred feet, skillfully avoiding the hills. The cleft in the trees grew wider, bringing the road into view.

"Look!" Joe yelled. "That's where our car turned over. The saplings we used for leverage are still there!"

"Start taking pictures," Frank ordered. "I'll keep an eye out for anything of special interest."

Joe gripped the camera and pointed it downward. Randy banked the plane so the young detective could take more direct aim. Joe made several exposures as the pilot circled the area, gradually widening his turns.

"I just spotted something!" Frank shouted.

"What is it?" Joe readied the camera.

"It looks like the roof of a small cabin," Frank replied. "If the sun weren't directly overhead, it would be hidden in the shadows. It's surrounded by trees and brush."

"I see it!" exclaimed Joe. He focused the camera and released the shutter.

"The cabin is near the spot where we saw Bush Barney," Frank declared.

"Do you think he could be hiding out there?" Joe questioned.

"It's possible. And perhaps our friend with the shotgun too!"

The pilot rolled out of the turn. "We'll fly straight and level for a few seconds," he said. "If we continue those tight turns for too long, we might get vertigo."

Their straight course took them over an area on the opposite side of the road. Frank suddenly noticed a rectangular-shaped field that looked like a pasture.

"Fly over that way," he said to Randy, pointing almost directly ahead.

The pilot eased the plane into a course around the narrow clearing. Frank and Joe saw that the grassy field was bordered by trees and dense brush. At one end loomed a high, steep hill.

"What do you make of it?" Frank asked, glancing at the pilot. "Do you think a small plane could land there, and take off?"

"I doubt it," Randy said. "But let's go down for a closer look-see."

He dropped the plane's nose steeply, pulling out over the clearing below tree level. He carefully dragged the field, then applied full power and turned sharply away from the steep hill ahead.

"That clearing is only about nine hundred feet long," he told the boys. "The approaches are very bad. I doubt whether anyone could get a plane in there without rolling it up into a ball. And even if a landing were possible, he'd never be able to take off again."

The boys' thoughts turned back to the airplane they had encountered on the road. If it had crashed, where was the wreckage? It must have pulled up and gone off. Did the roadblock and the red flare have something to do with the maneuver?

Frank took over with the camera. Quickly reloading it, he photographed the open area. Joe peered through his binoculars. Suddenly he snapped up in his seat.

"Down in the clearing!" he shouted. "See those two men stalking along the edge!"

The pilot banked the plane and lined up for another low pass. As they approached, Frank also spotted the two figures. Joe focused his binoculars more sharply.

"I'm not sure," he yelled excitedly, "but I think one of those men is Bush Barney!"

As the plane roared closer, the two men whirled around. They glanced up, then turned and ran into the woods.

"Quick!" Frank shouted to Randy. "Pull around and make another low pass!"

The pilot again pulled up steeply to turn away from the hill ahead. But just as he pushed the throttle forward for more power, the engine suddenly sputtered, then quit completely. Randy immediately dropped the nose in an effort to keep flying speed and avoid a stall.

The boys looked ahead. Through the windshield all they could see was a formidable array of trees, dense brush, and hills strewn with rocks and boulders. They tightened their seat belts and braced themselves for the worst. There was no place to land. They would have to crash!

CHAPTER VII

A Strange Request

RANDY Watson, his face grim, desperately switched fuel tanks. He pumped the throttle but the engine failed to react.

He put the plane into a gentle turn and headed down a narrow valley. The propeller slowly windmilled in the slipstream, as the anxious Hardys watched the ominous terrain rising steadily toward them.

The pilot continued to manipulate the fuel valves, mixture control, and throttle. Frank nervously glanced at the altimeter. They were rapidly losing altitude.

Finally Randy reached for a toggle switch marked "Booster Pump" and snapped it to the "On" position. He pumped the throttle vigorously. Suddenly the engine backfired—once, then twice. The boys held their breaths. There was a chugging sound for a few seconds! Then the engine roared to life.

Randy pushed the throttle to full power. Already the tops of trees were whipping against the plane, leaving green-colored streaks along the leading edges of the wings. The pilot eased back on the control stick and managed to pull away from the treetops. Ahead, he saw that the valley bent sharply to the right.

He banked the plane into a tight turn and followed the valley's course. It seemed to grow narrower second by second; the steep hills flanking each side squeezed closer. Randy checked the airspeed indicator, then raised the nose to gain altitude. Soon the hilltops were flashing by below them.

"Whew!" Joe exclaimed. "That was too close for comfort."

"What happened to the engine?" Frank asked the pilot.

"Fuel-pump failure, I think," Randy said. "Right now, we're operating on the booster. It's acting as a kind of auxiliary pump, and should keep the engine running long enough to get us back to Bayport."

During the return trip Frank removed the second roll of film from the camera, and placed it with the other one on the seat beside him. Eventually the airport came into view, and Randy radioed the control tower for a straight-in approach,

The boys could see an emergency truck stationed near the runway as they touched down.

A small crowd had already collected on the parking ramp as they taxied in. One of the group was Jerry Madden.

"What happened?" he queried anxiously.

"The pilot thinks it was fuel-pump failure," Frank answered.

"I heard him declare an emergency on the radio in the hangar," said Jerry. "When Lance Peterson heard you fellows were aboard, he asked to see you right away."

"Lance Peterson?" Frank said wonderingly. "He wants to see Joe and me?"

The Hardys were so amazed at hearing Peterson's request that they momentarily forgot about their photographing mission and near crash. They hurried immediately to the chief pilot's office.

When the brothers arrived, Peterson greeted them with a smile. His attitude had apparently undergone a complete change since they had met the first time.

"I hear you boys had a pretty close call," he remarked.

"Close enough!" Frank responded tersely. He was eager to find out why Peterson had asked to see them.

The chief pilot looked haggard and worried. He sat down and nervously tapped the top of his desk with a pencil.

"I learned only recently that you two are amateur detectives," he said.

"Yes, we are," Frank admitted. "But what has that to do with your asking to see us?"

"I want you to take a case for me," said Peterson. "Please don't refuse."

Frank and Joe were startled at the request. There was silence for a moment, then Frank spoke up. "What kind of case?"

Peterson spoke in a hushed voice. He repeated the story about the crash at sea in which Clint Hill had been lost.

"I was copilot on that trip, and the only survivor," he said.

"We know all that," Joe said impatiently.

Peterson's voice dropped almost to a whisper. The boys had difficulty hearing him.

"As pilot in command," he said—almost pleadingly, the boys thought—"Hill was responsible for the accident."

Peterson grew even more tense. Perspiration began to show on his face.

"But for some reason"—he went on in a quavering voice, then paused as he got up and came to stand directly in front of the boys—"Clint Hill has started to haunt me!"

"Haunt you?" Frank exclaimed. "In what way could a dead man haunt you?"

"Clint used to whistle a lot," said Peterson. "His

favorite tune was 'High Journey.' Now I keep hearing him whistle it—here, at home, over my plane radio. Sometimes he breaks off and laughs!"

"Are you sure somebody isn't just playing a joke on you?" Joe suggested.

"No!" the pilot answered. "A few days ago I heard him radio the tower for landing instructions. Then he flew off, saying, 'The dead can tell no tales.' It all came in clearly on my office radio receiver over there," he said, pointing to a box-shaped unit which stood on a table across the room. "I realize now you boys weren't joking."

"This is very unusual," said Frank. "But what can Joe and I do for you?"

"I know I'm not hearing things," Peterson stated. "Somebody is trying to drive me out of my mind, probably to get my job. I want you boys to find out who it is!"

"Chasing ghosts is a bit out of our line," Frank said. "We'll have to think it over."

Peterson appeared desperate. "I wish you would start on the case now," he said. "But if you must think it over, let me know as soon as you decide."

The Hardys left Peterson's office and started back to the Ace Air Service parking ramp. As they walked, the brothers discussed this new and puzzling development.

"I'd say he was off his rocker," commented Joe, "if it weren't for the fact that we too heard the voice of Clint Hill's ghost."

"Could be," said Frank. "But I don't go along with Peterson's idea that someone is trying to drive him out of his mind in order to get his job."

Joe agreed and asked Frank if he thought they should take the case. Frank replied that it would be best to discuss the matter with their father before making any decision.

As they arrived at the parking ramp, the young sleuths saw Randy Watson standing near the airplane with a mechanic.

"Find the trouble?" Frank called.

"It *was* the fuel pump that caused the engine to fail!" Randy replied.

"Thanks to your skill," Frank said with a smile, "we avoided becoming a permanent part of the landscape!"

Randy said he hoped the trip had not been a waste of time.

"Oh, no. We managed to get plenty of pictures before the engine quit," Frank answered. "Incidentally, we'd better get the films developed just as soon as possible," he said to Joe.

The young detectives climbed into the cabin of the plane. They were puzzled not to find the camera and containers of film where they had left them.

Frank shouted to Randy, who was standing on the ramp, "Did you take the camera and films into the operations building?"

"No," the pilot responded with a startled air. "Are you certain they're not in the cabin?"

The boys searched again, becoming more frantic with each second.

"Were you away from the plane at any time?" Frank asked Randy.

"Only for a few minutes when I went to get a mechanic."

The Hardys stared into the empty cabin.

"Those valuable pictures!" Frank burst out. "Our films! They've been stolen!"

CHAPTER VIII

Masked Attacker

THERE was a moment of thunderstruck silence. Who had stolen the Hardys' camera and films and why?

Randy was apologetic, saying he felt responsible for leaving the plane unattended. "I'll pay for the loss," he declared.

"We wouldn't consider it," Frank said, shaking his head. "Besides, it's not so much the camera we're worried about."

"The films?"

"Right," Joe added quickly. He cast a glance at his brother. "You probably have the same suspicion I do, Frank. The thief might have wanted to prevent us from developing those pictures."

"Then why did he take the camera too?" was Randy's next query.

"Because he figured there was more exposed film in it," Frank explained.

"Good reasoning," Randy agreed.

The boys recalled the small crowd that had collected on the ramp when their plane taxied in. Jerry Madden had been among them. Perhaps, Frank thought, he might know who some of the other onlookers were. The young detectives returned to the Stanwide hangar to question Jerry.

"I recognized only two faces in the crowd," said Jerry, after the boys told him about the theft. "Mike Zimm, the mechanic, and Aaron Lieber, a copilot mechanic, who seems to be a special pal of Lance Peterson's."

"Zimm again." Frank's eyes narrowed. "Odd, the way he keeps popping up in our case."

"Sure is," said Joe. "I'll bet that snoopy mechanic is somehow mixed up in the platinum business, but why would he want our films?"

The Hardys finally decided to trail Zimm and Lieber when the two men quit work for the day. Frank asked Jerry for a description of Lieber, then requested the pilot to check the men's lockers for the stolen camera.

"They keep them locked," Jerry said. "Everyone around here does. But the doors have slats a little wider than is usual. Maybe I can peer in through the openings. I'll try after Zimm and Lieber leave."

The Hardys hurried from the hangar. Frank hid behind some engine crates a short distance away. Joe, at his brother's direction, went to the airport terminal building to telephone Chet Morton and another friend, Biff Hooper. Their pals' help might come in handy if the Hardys ran into trouble while tailing Zimm and Lieber.

It was not long before Joe returned. "We're in luck," he said. "Chet can use his father's produce delivery truck, which will be a good cover-up. He's starting for the airport immediately, and will pick up Biff on the way. I told Chet to wait for us near our car in the visitors' parking lot."

Nearly half an hour passed before Zimm and a thin, bony-faced man with beady eyes emerged from the Stanwide hangar. "Aaron Lieber," muttered Frank. The young sleuths watched the men carefully. Neither of them carried anything, and the aerial camera was too bulky to be hidden beneath their coats. The pair stopped for a few minutes and talked in low tones, then got into separate cars and drove off.

Frank and Joe dashed to the visitors' parking lot. There they recognized the Mortons' farm truck and ran to it. Behind the wheel was the Hardys' stout chum, and seated next to him, was tall, lanky Biff Hooper. Biff was an energetic boy, who prided himself on his boxing ability.

"There's no time to lose!" Frank declared. "Joe, you go with Chet in the truck and follow Lieber. I'll take Biff with me in our car and tail Zimm!"

The two vehicles drove off and headed toward the airport exit, through which the two suspects would have had to pass. The boys' timing was perfect. They neared the exit just as the cars driven by Zimm and Lieber pulled out onto the main road.

After driving a short distance, the two men took different routes. Frank followed Zimm, dropping behind as far as possible so as not to be conspicuous. Joe and Chet went in pursuit of Lieber.

As Frank and Biff rode along, Frank briefly outlined the situation to his friend, who nodded enthusiastically. "You can count on me if there's any trouble." He set his jaw and skillfully executed several left jabs in the air.

"Save your energy," Frank told him with a grin. "You might need it."

The young sleuth kept his eyes fixed on the car ahead. As they entered town a short while later, he saw it slow down and stop. Zimm got out and went into a photographic shop. "Freeman's Camera House," Frank observed. He wondered if this was just a coincidence, or was Zimm planning to have the stolen films developed?

"When Zimm comes out," he told Biff, "you take the car and follow him. I want to question the shop owner."

"But when will we join up?" his friend asked.

Frank reached into his pocket and took out an

emergency detective kit. From it he extracted a packet containing small pieces of vivid red paper, and handed it to Biff.

"As you drive," he told him, "drop some of this paper every few seconds. That will leave a trail I can follow later."

"But what if I run out of paper?" Biff asked.

"If you have to follow Zimm that far," said Frank, "stay with him and find out where he goes. Then retrace your route. I'll be following the trail on foot for as far as it takes me.

"In the meantime," Frank went on, "I want to call Jerry Madden at the Stanwide hangar and ask him if he's had an opportunity to check the men's lockers."

Frank got out of the car. He found a public telephone across the street, where he was able to call and still keep an eye on the camera shop.

Summoned to the phone, Jerry Madden told Frank that he had found no sign of the aerial camera in either of the lockers. Frank requested Jerry to keep his eyes open and to call Mr. Hardy should anything turn up.

Frank had just completed the call when he saw Zimm come out of the shop and get into his car. He drove off, with Biff trailing behind.

Frank hurried into the camera shop. A man of medium height, with dark hair, was jotting notes in his order book. He proved to be the owner, Mr. Freeman.

The young detective identified himself, and asked if Mr. Zimm, who had just been there, had left film to be developed. Mr. Freeman said the man had left four rolls to be developed, but had given him the name R. C. Williams.

Frank realized that it was possible the films really did belong to a man named Williams, and that Zimm was merely having them developed for him. There would be no way of knowing until the pictures were developed.

"Mr. Freeman," said Frank, "we Hardys are suspicious these are films that were stolen from us."

The proprietor was eager to help the boys find out. He promised that when the negatives and prints were returned from the laboratory he would notify Frank immediately.

"Thanks a lot," Frank said, then left the shop. Daylight was beginning to fade, prompting him to hurry in search of the trail he had instructed Biff to mark. Almost immediately, he spotted the first bit of red paper. Then another piece, and another.

Frank estimated that he had walked nearly a mile when the trail led him onto a quiet residential street. He quickened his pace as darkness increased and a breeze sprang up, threatening to erase the paper trail. Dead ahead, he was suddenly elated to see his car parked on the street. As Frank neared it, he could see Biff at the wheel.

"How did things work out?" Frank asked in a

low voice, as he eased into the seat beside his pal.

"Luckily your suspect reached his destination before I ran out of paper," Biff said.

He pointed to a house a short distance away and told Frank that Zimm was inside.

"He lives there," said Biff. "I got out and walked past the house. His name plate is posted on the lawn."

Frank said that he wanted to watch the house a while. "Biff, how about your driving to the nearest store and picking up some sandwiches, milk, and ice cream for us? We may be here a long time."

Biff went off and Frank stationed himself behind a tree. Daylight was now completely gone. The area was quiet, and light radiation fog was beginning to drift from the trees and shrubbery. Frank folded his arms against a chill that was developing in the air. He hoped that Biff would not be too long getting back.

Suddenly the stillness was disturbed by the sound of someone whistling. It seemed to be coming from the far side of Zimm's house. Frank recognized the tune.

"High Journey!"

An eerie feeling gripped him. Was he hearing the ghost of Clint Hill?

The young detective bent low, crossed the street, and carefully edged toward the house. The sound, he was now certain, was coming from the far side of the dwelling. Frank slowly crept to the rear and listened. The whistle was louder now. He braced himself, then broke into a fast sprint.

As Frank rounded the corner of the house, he suddenly collided with a tall man. The force of the contact threw both of them to the ground. Dazed for a second, Frank took a deep breath, then scrambled to his feet.

The stranger also got up. He was wearing a mask! The man turned to run, but Frank was too fast for him. He managed to catch him by the collar. As the two tumbled and rolled across the ground, the stranger swung his fist.

Frank received a hard body blow that badly stunned him. The stranger leaped to his feet and ran. Frank made an effort to pursue him, but was too late. With consternation, he watched the masked figure vanish into the darkness.

CHAPTER IX

Alley Escape

MEANWHILE, Joe and Chet had followed Aaron Lieber to his apartment house. It was a small stone building with doors to the outside at both the front and rear.

They parked the truck half a block beyond it and hurried back. Joe quickly scrutinized the premises. Then he assigned Chet to guard the rear door, while he himself would watch the front.

"If Lieber has our camera hidden in his apartment, he may sneak it out," Joe told him, "so keep your eyes open."

"Okay," Chet answered. "Say, this kind of work sure can give a man an appetite," he hinted.

Joe knew that once his chum had felt the pangs of hunger, it was hopeless to try taking his mind off food. It took little prompting to send Chet rushing off to get both of them something to eat.

The young detective watched both the front

door and the service alley of the apartment house. No one came out, and it was not long before his stout pal reappeared carrying sandwiches, cartons of chocolate milk, and fruit.

He handed Joe an apple. "This will do for an appetizer," he announced.

Chet then divided the rest of the food and carried his portion down the narrow alleyway to take up his post at the rear door of the building.

Actually, Chet found two doors there. One was located at the top of a short iron stairway and led into the first floor of the apartment house.

The second, which obviously led to the basement, was situated directly below the other. Chet looked around and selected a vantage point in the shadow of an adjacent building.

"Guess nobody can see me here," he thought.

As Chet began munching on his third sandwich, his eyes suddenly focused on the upper door. It was, he realized, being eased open. The figure of a man carrying a large package under his arm slowly emerged. Closing the door quietly behind him, he crept down the stairway.

"The camera!" Chet decided.

He bolted from the shadow of the building. The man spotted him immediately. Startled, the stranger turned and broke into a fast run up the alleyway toward the street. Chet took off after him, still holding his sandwich and carton of chocolate milk.

The distance between Chet and the man he was pursuing rapidly closed. In desperation, the stranger stopped and whirled about. Chet was caught off guard.

"You—you—!" the man hissed at him.

Holding the package with one hand, he reached out with the other and wrenched the carton of milk from Chet's grasp. Then he threw its contents full force into the boy's face!

"That'll teach you!" the man snarled.

Chet was blinded by the deluge. He stood sputtering, vigorously wiping the liquid from his eyes. By the time he could see again, the man had disappeared.

In disgust Chet dashed out of the alleyway and around to the front entrance of the apartment house, to warn Joe. No one was there! The farm truck was gone.

Chet was in a quandary. Not only had the stranger disappeared, but so had Joe!

"Perhaps," Chet thought, "Joe spotted the man running from the alley with the package and drove after him. I sure hope so."

The stout boy took up a position across the street from the apartment house. From there, he could watch for Joe and guard the front of the building at the same time. The only people he saw come out were two women carrying small handbags. He observed nothing suspicious.

Finally Joe pulled up in the truck and hopped

"That'll teach you!" the man snarled

out. Chet ran to meet him. "I was beginning to worry," said the plump boy. "Where did you go?"

"While watching from here, I saw a man running out of the alley," Joe answered. "He was Lieber! Before I could catch him, he jumped into a car parked up the street. I chased him in your truck, but I got mixed up in a traffic jam and lost him."

Chet told Joe about his encounter with Lieber, and pointed to his chocolate-stained clothes. He apologized for having been caught by surprise.

"It couldn't be helped," Joe excused him. "The car that Lieber jumped into was waiting for him, I'm sure. I managed to get the license plate number. We can check it out tomorrow with the motor vehicle department."

By now the boys were convinced that there was little to be gained by continuing to watch the apartment house, so they decided to go home.

"What do you think Lieber was up to?" Chet asked as they rode through the Bayport streets.

"I don't know," Joe responded. "But whatever it was, he certainly wasn't wasting any time."

"Do you think that was the camera he was carrying?" Chet questioned.

"Yes. Some pal might have sneaked it from the airport to Lieber's place. We have no proof, though."

Chet stopped at the Hardy house and dropped

Joe off. Then he sped for home, his face beaming with anticipation of the hearty meal he knew would be waiting for him.

Joe was about to enter the house when he saw Frank turn into the driveway. "Hi!" he called.

"Did you just get back?" Frank asked as he climbed out of the convertible.

"Yes. Did you have any luck following Zimm?"

"Enough to make me more suspicious of him," Frank replied. "I'll put the car in the garage and then let's talk."

In a few moments the boys went into the house. Mrs. Hardy and Aunt Gertrude were relieved to see them, since it was long past dinnertime.

"You must be starved," Aunt Gertrude remarked. "And besides, the food's half ruined, standing here for over an hour!"

Mrs. Hardy smiled. "I don't think the boys will mind."

The boys did not mind. They found the roast lamb, mashed potatoes, peas, and strawberry short-cake delicious. All the Hardys laughed over Joe's description of Chet's encounter with Lieber and the chocolate milk.

After dinner the brothers joined their father in his study. Frank was the first to tell his story, then Joe. Mr. Hardy listened with great interest.

"You say the man who knocked you down wore a mask?" he asked Frank.

"Yes! And if he was a ghost, he was a pretty solid one! By the way, Peterson has asked us to find the ghost! Shall we take his case?"

Mr. Hardy thought for several seconds before answering. "Yes, take it. This so-called ghost seems to bob up a good deal. He's worth pursuing."

The detective and his sons also agreed that the mysterious behavior of Zimm and Lieber could not be coincidence. It must be linked with the case, and the two were working together in some sinister plot.

Mr. Hardy warned his sons that they should be extra careful. "If Zimm and Lieber are involved in the platinum thefts, and think you suspect them, they may make it sticky for you."

"We'll try not to flub again," Frank promised.

"What do you plan to do next?" their father inquired.

"I'd like to drive out to Zimm's house tomorrow morning," Frank replied, "and investigate the area. We might be able to come up with a clue or two."

"Good idea. I'll keep on investigating at Stanwide itself."

Early the next day Frank and Joe drove to Zimm's house and cruised slowly past it. They saw that the garage, in which Zimm kept his car, was empty, and surmised that he had already left for work. The boys parked their car on the next block, then walked back toward the house. They tried to act nonchalant.

"That's where I ran into the masked stranger," Frank said, pointing. "You investigate that side of the house, and I'll reconnoiter the grounds."

Frank scanned the premises carefully, inch by inch. He saw the area of ruffled grass where he and the masked stranger had tumbled in their struggle. Unfortunately, even his trained eyes failed to detect a single clue.

As Frank continued the examination, his brother suddenly spotted something which startled him.

"For Pete's sake!" Joe exclaimed.

CHAPTER X

Startling Discoveries

FRANK rushed over to Joe. His brother was staring at something in a flower bed. Frank glanced down and was astonished at what he saw. There, deeply impressed in the soft dirt, were two footprints.

The instep of the right foot was narrower than that of the left. The prints appeared to be duplicates of those the boys had discovered in the concrete floor of the Stanwide hangar.

Clint Hill's footprints!

"What do you make of it?" Joe asked his brother excitedly. "Could Clint Hill be alive?"

"The reports certainly don't indicate it," Frank replied. "But if he is, why would he be sneaking around like this?"

"I wonder if the whole thing is a hoax," Joe said. "Maybe Lance Peterson is using us to cover up a crooked deal he and Hill are involved in.

They feel safe because they didn't count on our picking up the footprint clue in the hangar. Someone tried hard to keep us from seeing the prints. Maybe it was Hill himself!"

Puzzled, the boys decided to have another talk with Peterson. As they were about to leave, a window in the house was flung open, and a woman poked her head out.

"What are you doing here?" she shouted.

Startled, the boys looked up. "We wanted to see Mr. Zimm. Is he at home?" Frank replied coolly.

"Then why didn't you come to the door, instead of prowling around out there?" demanded the woman in a rasping, unpleasant tone. "I'm Mrs. Zimm. What do you want with my husband?"

The Hardys realized that they could not reveal to Mrs. Zimm their reasons for being there. Perhaps she was in the plot with her husband! On the other hand, she might not know anything about his mysterious behavior, nor have heard any talk about Clint Hill's ghost. In that case, the boys did not want to upset her.

"We're working on a job for Lance Peterson," Joe ad-libbed, "and we wanted to ask Mr. Zimm some questions."

"He left for work about an hour ago," his wife said indignantly.

"Then we'll see him there," Frank told her.

She demanded that the boys leave at once. Glad to get away, they did not argue and returned to their car. Frank started for the Stanwide hangar.

"I could see by her face that Mrs. Zimm didn't know whether to believe us or not," Frank commented.

Joe agreed. "I hope that when she tells Zimm we were here, it doesn't put him on guard."

"It won't make much difference one way or the other," Frank observed. "Either Zimm knows we suspect him of something—which means our prowling around wouldn't surprise him—or else he might really believe we came out to ask him some routine questions."

When the boys arrived at the airport, they went at once to the Stanwide hangar. Lance Peterson's office door was locked. As Frank and Joe strolled back across the hangar, they saw Jerry Madden come out of the operations room.

"I've got a message for you!" he called to the Hardys. "Mr. Allen has been trying to find you. He wants you to call him right away."

Frank asked Jerry if he knew where Peterson had gone. Jerry said No, Peterson had taken the day off. Frank went to telephone Mr. Allen.

"We are sending a large shipment of parts containing platinum to the Sun-Plat Tool Company in California tomorrow morning," the executive told him. "Our company cargo plane will make the delivery. Lance Peterson and Aaron Lieber will be flying it. Because of the great value of this shipment, and the trouble we've been having, as an extra precaution I would like you boys to follow in another plane. Can you do it?"

The Hardys excitedly agreed. "Don't worry about arranging for a pilot and plane—we'll handle that ourselves," Frank said.

A short time later he and Joe were in the operations room of Ace Air Service, discussing the trip with Randy Watson.

"The Stanwide cargo plane is a pretty fast ship," Randy said. "We don't have any equipment at Ace that would keep up with her. I'll have to lease a special plane."

"Go ahead and make the arrangements," Frank told him. "But keep it quiet."

On the way home the Hardys stopped at police headquarters to ask them to check the license plate number of the car Joe had seen Lieber jump into. Detective Lieutenant Obels, a determined but pleasant man, sent the number to the motor vehicle department by police teletype. In a little less than an hour Lieutenant Obels called the boys at their home.

"Here it is!" the officer announced. "The report says the car belongs to a Mr. Art Rodax."

Frank thanked the detective, then hung up. "Art Rodax, our former boss!" he exclaimed, repeating the news to Joe.

"Good night! He's a pal of Lieber!" Joe cried out. "Well, we're rounding up quite a group of suspects!"

Hoping to turn up another clue, the boys began calling all the camera stores listed in the telephone book. Not one of the shops reported having seen the stolen camera.

At five o'clock Mr. Freeman called Frank. The camera-shop owner said that the developed pictures had just arrived. "Mr. Williams, the name under which the pictures were left, has already telephoned that he's coming by for them."

"We'll be right over," said Frank. "If Williams shows up first, try to stall him."

"Okay."

When the boys drove up to the camera shop, they saw a large, burly man who seemed to be arguing with Mr. Freeman.

"That isn't Zimm!" observed Joe. "Maybe he really does have a friend named Williams and he was delivering the rolls of film for him."

"Possibly," Frank agreed. "Then again, it might all be part of a clever plan to throw us off the track."

The boys decided to demand a chance to inspect the films. As they entered the shop, Mr. Freeman turned to them with an air of relief.

"This is Mr. R. C. Williams," he said, indicating his customer. Then he turned back to the man. "These boys believe that at least some of these pictures belong to them."

"What!" shouted Williams. "That's crazy!"

"Then you won't mind if we have a look at the prints," Frank said politely.

"Touch my pictures," Williams bellowed, "and I'll sue every one of you!"

Mr. Freeman looked hesitant. He was thinking that perhaps the Hardys were being a bit hasty. At the thought of being involved in a lawsuit, he began to hedge.

"Maybe we have no right to ask Mr. Williams to—" he began.

"We'll take the entire responsibility," Frank interrupted. "Mr. Williams can show us the pictures himself. We won't touch them."

Williams protested strongly. But seeing that the boys were determined not to let him out of the shop without seeing the pictures, he ripped open the big envelope, peered in, selected a few prints, and scattered them on the counter. None of the pictures belonged to the Hardys, they admitted.

"There!" Williams sneered. "You see? You guys ought to be thrown in jail!"

He quickly gathered up the prints and stuffed them back into the envelope.

"How much do I owe you?" he snapped at Mr. Freeman.

"Just a minute!" Frank said coldly. "We want to see *all* the pictures!"

"Get out of my way!" Williams shouted.

The shop owner, now more suspicious of Williams himself, offered to call the police. But at the word "police," Williams paled.

"You won't have to do that!" he blurted. Reluctantly he reached into the package and displayed several more prints.

"I said we want to see all of them!" Frank demanded.

"That's all there are," Williams insisted.

Joe reached out and seized the envelope. Shaking it vigorously, he spilled more prints onto the counter. The boys were elated to find that their suspicions were justified. Among the pictures were several aerial views they had taken!

Suddenly Williams let fly with his fists. He caught Mr. Freeman under the chin, and the shop owner slumped down behind the counter. Williams then whirled around and rushed the boys with his head down and arms flailing.

Frank and Joe, taken off guard, skidded on the highly polished floor and went down. Williams grabbed the pictures in his large fist and crammed them hastily into a pocket.

As the boys sprang to their feet, they saw Williams fleeing toward the rear exit of the shop!

CHAPTER XI

A Questionable Friend

FRANK and Joe darted after Williams and succeeded in intercepting him before he reached the rear exit. A wild struggle followed.

The boys and their burly opponent crashed to the floor in a mass of entangled arms and legs. Mr. Freeman, having recovered from the blow he had received, rushed over to give his support. Williams was exceptionally strong, but three against one was too much for him.

"That's enough!" he panted. "Don't hit me again!" He dropped and lay on the floor like a whipped dog.

"You'd better do some explaining!" Frank said angrily as he and Joe stood up and brushed off their clothing.

Joe grabbed the envelope and extracted several pictures. "The aerial shots!" he exclaimed, and handed them to his brother.

"I've nothing to say," growled Williams, trying to catch his breath. He sat up and ran a hand through his hair.

"Who stole our camera and films?" Frank demanded, glaring at their captive.

"I don't know about anything being stolen!" Williams insisted.

"Okay! Have it your way!" Frank declared. "Maybe you'd rather talk to the police!" The young sleuth walked to the telephone and began dialing a number.

Williams turned pale. "No! Wait!" he pleaded. "I'll tell you all I know! Honest I will. Don't call them!"

Frank put down the phone. "Go ahead!" he ordered.

"My name isn't Williams. It's Richard Tyson," the man said, taking out his wallet. He displayed his driver's license and a few credit cards.

The boys examined the cards and found the man's address was the same as that of the apartment house in which Lieber lived.

"Then who is Williams?" Frank asked.

"Williams rents a room across the hall from my apartment," Tyson answered. "Early this morning he asked me if I would pick up his pictures when they were ready. He told me to use his name.

"He explained that the pictures were confidential and not to let anyone see them. I'm sorry now I ever agreed to do it. I should have suspected something phony." He got to his feet, brushed himself off, and looked at the boys nervously. "I'd like to leave," he said, moving toward the door.

"Not until you tell us everything," said Frank. "Who stole our camera?"

"I told you I don't know."

"Does Williams live alone?"

"No, he rents the room from Mr. and Mrs. Lieber. The Liebers seem like nice people. I think Williams is Mrs. Lieber's brother."

The Hardys did not disclose that Mr. Lieber was already one of their strong suspects in the case.

"Well," Frank announced, "you can leave, but we're going with you to your apartment. We want to check your story."

"By all means! Come along!" Tyson urged. He seemed eager for a chance to prove his innocence.

Frank asked Mr. Freeman to put the aerial pictures in his safe until the boys called for them. "We don't want to risk their being stolen again."

The brothers took Tyson with them, explaining that they would bring him back later to pick up his own car. As they drove, Tyson volunteered the information that Lieber was an airplane mechanic and stand-by copilot. As a result, he was away a lot. In fact, he often slept at the airport.

In a short time the group arrived at the apartment house. Tyson unlocked the main door with his own key. As they climbed the stairs, Frank said that he would like to find out whether Lieber was at home.

Tyson pointed to the door of the man's apartment and Frank knocked. The door opened, revealing a stocky, handsome woman, with a tremendous amount of blond hair.

"Hello, Mr. Tyson," she said, seeing her neighbor.

"Is Mr. Lieber at home?" Frank inquired.

"No," she responded. "My husband has to fly very early tomorrow, so he decided to stay overnight at the airport."

"Is Mr. Williams at home?" Joe asked.

"He's not here, either," the woman said. "Is it anything important? Can I take a message?"

"No, thank you."

Mrs. Lieber eased the door shut. Tyson led the Hardys to his apartment across the hall. There they met Mrs. Tyson, a short, middle-aged woman. She invited them to come in.

Frank casually conversed with her, selecting his words in such a way that the woman was not aware that he was probing for information. She told the young sleuth that Mrs. Lieber was a very secretive person who seemed extremely frightened of her husband.

"She tries to forget her worries," Mrs. Tyson said confidingly, "by always going to the movies and to parties. Poor thing. The Liebers never have any company."

Momentarily satisfied with Tyson's story, the Hardys drove the man back to the camera shop to pick up his car. He said little more to shed any new light on the mystery and was obviously relieved when the boys drove off.

When they reached home, Frank and Joe discussed the information they had gathered that day. "I'm convinced," said Frank, "that Lieber and this Williams are mixed up in the Stanwide case."

"So far, nearly all our suspects are company employees," Joe commented. "How does this fellow Williams figure in?"

"It's possible that he's part of the racket, but working from the outside," Frank suggested.

The boys recalled Jerry Madden's remark about Lieber's being Peterson's pal. They wondered if this meant that the chief pilot himself was involved in the thefts.

"And it doesn't surprise me that Art Rodax fits into the picture," said Joe. "I knew he had a secret reason for not wanting us around the plant."

At that moment the telephone rang. The caller was Randy Watson. The pilot said that he had managed to rent an aircraft suitable for a long-distance flight from an operator at Lockwood Airport. This field was about two hundred miles from Bayport.

"I've already been there and flown the plane

back," he said. "She checks out fine. We'll be ready to roll any time in the morning."

"Good," Frank answered. "Joe and I will be at the airport early. We can't risk missing Peterson and Lieber's departure."

At dinner the boys packed some light luggage. Mrs. Hardy and Aunt Gertrude tried to hide their anxiety when they heard the coming flight was to trail Peterson and Lieber, but an expression of concern crossed Mrs. Hardy's face.

"Don't take any unnecessary chances," she begged. "And keep in constant touch with us."

Frank and Joe promised to do this. They assured the women that the trip was only routine, and that they would be away not more than two or three days.

"Two or three days!" Aunt Gertrude exclaimed. "If you catch those thieves the first day, why can't you come home? That's where you belong, anyway!"

The boys grinned and Joe said, "Why, Aunty, the longer the chase the more fun."

"Fun nothing!" she stormed. "A lot of danger—unnecessary danger for a couple of growing boys!" Miss Hardy's tirade ended only because she was called to the telephone.

Mr. Hardy, on the other hand, made no objection to the trip. "Best of luck, boys," he said.

The following morning the boys started for the airport as soon as dawn broke. When they arrived, the Hardys spotted a sleek, highly polished twin-engine turbo-prop plane parked on the Ace Air Service ramp.

"That must be the plane Randy rented!" Joe exclaimed, pointing. "My, what a beauty! Wish I could fly her!"

Frank grinned in anticipation. "It sure looks as if we won't have any trouble keeping up with Peterson in that!"

The boys put down their bags and approached the plane for a closer look. Just then Randy Watson came running out of the operations building.

"Hey, fellows!" he shouted excitedly. "Come here, quick!"

The young detectives ran to meet him.

"What is it?" Frank called. "Something wrong?"

"I just tried to phone you at home," Randy answered, "but you had already left. It's about the Stanwide cargo plane!"

"What happened?" Joe asked.

"Peterson and Lieber left hours ago!" Randy said, trying to catch his breath. "They took off late last night!"

CHAPTER XII

The Cave Clue

THE Hardy boys wasted no time. Moments later, they were dashing up the circular stairs to the Bayport control tower.

"Is Lou Diamond here?" Frank asked as they burst into the room.

"No," answered a lean, middle-aged man, who was seated at a desk. "The chief doesn't come on duty for another hour yet."

The brothers explained the situation to him and requested his help.

"I remember the Stanwide plane taking off," the tower man recalled. "It departed soon after I came on duty." He quickly checked through his listing of aircraft movements. "Here it is," he said, pointing out a small card. "The plane took off shortly after midnight."

"Did the pilot file a flight plan?" Frank questioned.

"Yes—an instrument flight plan to a field in California," the operator responded. "I can't tell you exactly, because normally we don't keep a record of flight plans here in the tower." He picked up a telephone and snapped a toggle switch mounted on the desk. "I'll check with our communications station."

It was several minutes before the operator received the information he requested. Then he placed the phone down and turned to the young sleuths. "The Stanwide pilot canceled his flight plan at Chicago," he said. "After taking on fuel, he departed without filing a new flight plan."

Frank and Joe were dismayed. After thanking the tower man for his help, they left hurriedly.

"I want to call Mr. Allen right away and let him know what happened," Frank said.

Mr. Allen's voice was heavy with sleep as he answered the telephone. When he heard the news, however, he snapped awake.

"What!" he exclaimed. "Peterson didn't have authority to leave before the scheduled time. Meet me at the Stanwide hangar! I'll be right over!"

The boys next called their father and informed him of the incident. Then they started walking toward the Stanwide hangar.

"Peterson and Lieber decided to vanish and keep everything for themselves," Frank said. "That was a valuable load they were carrying. It could make them rich."

"Peterson might also be trying to escape Clint Hill's ghost," Joe added.

Mr. Allen arrived at the hangar and was aghast at the situation. He immediately placed a long-distance call to the Sun-Plat Tool Company in California, which was supposed to receive the air shipment. An official there told him the cargo plane had not arrived at the nearby airport. He assured Mr. Allen he would notify him the instant any information concerning the flight was received.

Turning from the telephone, Mr. Allen said to the Hardys, "I don't mind telling you I'm pretty worried about this whole thing."

The boys followed him to Peterson's office, which they thoroughly searched. In the top desk drawer, Frank discovered a notation stating that Mr. Allen had ordered an earlier departure.

"I never gave such an order!" the executive declared. The young sleuths noted that the notation was typed, making it difficult to identify the writer.

They next went with Mr. Allen to interrogate the night watchman, who said Peterson had told him nothing. "I thought it was a funny time for him to be taking off, but it's not up to me to question the actions of our company's chief pilot."

"No, of course not," said Mr. Allen.

Using a master key, he searched Lieber's locker

but found no clues. Frank suggested they check the bills of lading for the Sun-Plat shipment. They scrutinized the records for more than an hour, but the results gave no hint of any tampering.

"Well," Frank said, sighing, "there's nothing more we can do here."

After assuring Mr. Allen they would continue tracking every possible lead locally, the Hardys returned to Randy.

"Sorry our flight has been grounded," Joe said wryly.

"Too bad. Well, I'll just return the plane," the pilot replied philosophically. "I'll be around if you fellows need me again—maybe next time we'll have better luck."

The boys, feeling somewhat let down, drove off. Frank suggested they go to the camera shop and examine the photographs Mr. Freeman was keeping for them.

"It's a long shot," he said, "but maybe those pictures will tell us something."

The boys arrived just as Mr. Freeman was opening his shop. He went to the wall safe, opened it, and handed them the negatives and prints. Joe picked up a magnifying glass from the counter. Mr. Freeman handed Frank another.

Meticulously the Hardys studied each of the aerial photographs. Several minutes passed before Joe suddenly cried out, "Look at this!"

Frank took the print and peered at it through

his glass. Joe pointed to the rectangular pasture over which they had flown low before the engine of their aircraft had failed. "What do you see in the pasture area?"

Frank moved his magnifying glass slowly for a better focus. "I don't notice anything special," he announced. "Unless you mean those three parallel lines running through the center of the pasture. They appear to be ruts, or grooves."

"Exactly!" Joe said. "What are they?"

"The lines could have been made by a three-wheeled farm tractor," Frank answered.

"Or maybe a small airplane!" Joe suggested.

"I wonder," said Frank, then added, "Randy Watson told us the pasture was too short for *any* airplane to operate out of."

"I know. That's what has me baffled."

Mr. Freeman, who had been watching the boys with interest, began glancing at some of the photographs. He asked in what locality the pictures had been taken. When the Hardys told him, his face broke into a wide smile.

"I thought I recognized the area," he remarked. "When I was a boy, spelunking was one of my favorite pastimes. I used to go there a lot."

"Spelunking?" Frank asked curiously. "You mean you went exploring caves in that area?"

"Oh, yes," Mr. Freeman answered, obviously pleased at recollecting some of his childhood activities. "There are several fine caves to be found in those hills. However, it's been so many years since I was there, I wouldn't be able to locate any of them now."

"How large are the caves?" Frank asked, with increasing interest.

"The ones I explored were rather small," the shop owner explained. "I promised my parents I wouldn't tackle anything too deep. So I can't say just how large the bigger caves are."

The boys thanked Mr. Freeman for his help, then started for home. Both were excited at learning of caves being in the area where they had seen Bush Barney. Perhaps, they speculated, the thieves were using a cave to hide their loot!

"There might even be one near the pasture we flew over!" Joe exclaimed. "And if I'm right about the deep grooves having been made by the wheels of a small plane, maybe it's possible the pasture is being utilized as a makeshift runway after all!"

"I have an idea!" said Frank. "Why don't we rent a helicopter and get a really close look at that area? But first let's go home and tell the folks about our change of plans."

Mrs. Hardy was elated to see her sons and to learn that their plane trip had been canceled.

Aunt Gertrude wore a self-satisfied grin. "Good thing," she said. "Now you boys will have time for a lunch that will make up for the breakfast you raced through this morning."

The Hardy family sat down to a meal of delicious homemade soup, followed by hamburgers, then gingerbread topped with applesauce and whipped cream. While they were eating, Frank and Joe related their conversation with Mr. Freeman, and told of their theory concerning a cavern hideout.

Mr. Hardy was interested at once. "A cave would be perfect for storing stolen merchandise," he agreed. "Incidentally, I've learned that tract of land is part of an abandoned farm, but the whereabouts of the owner is not known."

The boys discussed their plan to explore the area by helicopter. Their father approved, and suggested that they ask Randy Watson to make arrangements for hiring a craft and pilot.

Frank was about to make the call when the telephone rang. He picked it up. An eerie voice at the other end said, "Is this the Hardys' house?"

"Hi, Chet!" Frank said with a chuckle. His friend was imitating Clint Hill's voice.

But as the unearthly voice continued, Frank realized it was not Chet's! The words it spoke turned his blood cold.

"*This is not Chet,*" intoned the speaker. "*This is the ghost of Clint Hill. Where is Lance Peterson?*"

CHAPTER XIII

The Tornado

CHILLS ran up and down Frank's spine and he stood motionless. He was about to answer that he did not know the whereabouts of Peterson, but then his momentary fright left him and he changed his mind. Frank decided to question the mysterious caller and perhaps get a lead as to his identity.

"I'll make a bargain with you," the young sleuth proposed.

"What kind of bargain?" asked the voice, still in an eerie tone.

"I'll give you some information about Peterson," said Frank, "if you'll tell me who you really are."

There was a long pause.

"Forget it!" said the sepulchral voice. *"I'll find that double-crosser myself!"*

"Wait!" Frank urged. "Don't hang up!"

But a sharp clicking sound brought the conversation to an abrupt end. Disappointed, Frank shrugged, then dialed and made arrangements to rent a helicopter. In a few minutes he rejoined his family. They discussed the weird call from the "ghost."

Mrs. Hardy looked distressed, while Aunt Gertrude expressed contempt. "These people who play tricks on the telephone!"

"You say that this person called Lance Peterson a double-crosser?" Mr. Hardy asked.

"That's right, Dad," Frank answered. "I wonder if our 'ghost' actually is in cahoots with Peterson and Lieber, and was supposed to go with them aboard the plane, then found they'd suddenly left without him."

Father and sons continued to discuss this new development and its connection with the case, but failed to arrive at any conclusion. Presently Randy Watson telephoned and said he had made arrangements for Frank and Joe to fly in a helicopter the following morning. A minute later Mr. Allen called to tell the boys that authorities in the United States, Canada, and Mexico had been alerted to look for the missing company plane.

"As yet nothing has been reported," he said.

The next day Frank and Joe went to Bayport Airport. As they walked onto the parking ramp of

Ace Air Service, Randy met the brothers and introduced them to Mack Carney, their pilot, young and well-built. A short distance away stood a small, three-place helicopter. Its cockpit was enclosed in a fishbowl-shaped Plexiglas canopy.

As the boys walked toward the craft, they glanced at the sky and noticed that a cloud cover was developing. Conditions to the south and southwest appeared especially bad. There, the bases of some clouds were darkening to an almost bluish black.

"Looks like a storm," Joe commented. He feared that their flight might be delayed because of weather.

"There shouldn't be any problem," Mack reassured him. "I've already checked the forecast. Ceilings and visibility are not expected to drop below visual flight rules at any time."

He told the Hardys that scattered thunderstorms were predicted for the area, but that these could easily be avoided. By midafternoon the weather system was expected to move out to sea, with rapid clearing behind it.

Minutes later, the helicopter was aloft. The loud clapping of the whirling rotor blades, mixed with the noise of the engine's muffler, bothered them for a few minutes. But gradually, as the craft gained height, turned and headed northwest, they ceased to think about it. The brothers settled back to enjoy the unobstructed view offered by the transparent canopy, and to watch the pilot.

"I'd like to learn to fly one of these," Joe commented.

The flight took a bit longer than their previous trip to the area by airplane. As they flew into the sector they wanted to investigate, Frank scanned the ground below. He spotted the pasture in the aerial photograph and pointed it out to Mack. The pilot bent the helicopter into a series of turns around the field.

As he leveled the craft out on an easterly heading, Joe glanced to his right. Suddenly the boy detective sat rigid in his seat and stared from the window with an expression of disbelief.

"Look!" he shouted frantically.

The pilot spun the helicopter around to face in the direction Joe was pointing. Moving toward them was a black, funnel-shaped column of air, stemming from the base of an intensely dark cloud.

"It looks like a tornado!" Frank yelled.

"It is!" Mack exclaimed. "They generally move in a northeasterly direction, about thirty to forty miles an hour. We might be able to outrun it."

He whirled the craft around, but was greatly alarmed to find that their route of escape was blocked by the surrounding hills. The dark cloud base moving swiftly overhead cut off the possibil-

"The tornado's getting closer!" Joe shouted

ity of climbing out over the top of the higher terrain.

"What'll we do? That tornado is getting closer!" Joe shouted.

"We'll have to head for the ground!" the pilot replied grimly.

As the menacing funnel approached, the surrounding air became turbulent. Mack struggled with the controls as the craft was thrown about viciously. Frank and Joe braced themselves as best they could, while the pilot tried to establish a controlled descent.

Suddenly Frank and Joe looked out to see a strange phenomenon. The funnel-shaped column seemed to divide in half, as if sliced by an invisible knife. The upper half veered off in a northeasterly direction, while the lower half maintained its original path, passing close to the bobbing helicopter.

"I'm losing control!" Mack shouted. "Hang on! We must be close to the ground!"

The violent jolt of landing almost knocked the helicopter's occupants unconscious. They sat dazed for several minutes before regaining their senses.

Then, gradually, the three became aware of a complete calm. The tornado and dark cloud had disappeared, and not even a breeze was stirring. The sky showed signs of clearing.

"Wow!" said Joe. "I hope that never happens to me again!"

"We're lucky to have got out of this in one piece," Mack said grimly.

He got out of the helicopter, followed by the Hardys, and began to examine the craft for damage. The boys, glancing around, realized that they had landed on a corner of the pasture.

"How's the copter?" Frank asked.

"The landing gear is sprung, and there's some structural damage here and there," Mack observed. "It doesn't appear to be serious, but I'd better give the craft a thorough inspection before we attempt to fly it out of here."

Frank and Joe decided to investigate the area while the pilot conducted his inspection. They started walking down the pasture toward the high hill situated at the far end.

"Here are those grooves we saw in our photos," Frank remarked. "They go from one end of the field to the other."

He took a tape measure from his pocket and carefully noted the width of the grooves and the distance between them. Pulling out a pencil, he jotted down the figures in his notebook for future reference.

"I still think these grooves were made by the wheels of an airplane," said Joe.

"But how? The length of the pasture rules out

the possibility that a plane could land here," Frank objected.

The boys continued heading for the hill at the far end. Just short of the tree line they stopped and peered into the murky shadows of the woods. The hill began to slope sharply upward at this point.

"I don't see any caves around here," Joe observed.

The boys were about to proceed closer when suddenly a man darted out from the woods. The boys recognized him immediately as the stranger who had previously challenged them near this spot. He was now unarmed.

"What are you doing here?" he bellowed. "Get off of this land! It's private property!"

"We were forced down by a storm," said Joe, pointing toward the helicopter just visible in the distance.

"The storm is over!" the man retorted. "Now you'd better climb into that bird and get out of here!"

"But we don't know if we *can* take off," said Frank. "We got bounced around pretty bad in the storm. The copter was damaged—how much, we don't know. Our pilot is inspecting it now."

"If it won't fly, you'll just have to leave it!" the man growled, his face purpling with anger. "I want you to get out of here—and fast!"

Meanwhile, out of the corner of his eye, Joe glimpsed a flicker of movement in the woods. He turned his head cautiously in an effort to get a better view. What he saw caused him to grab his brother's arm as a signal not to argue further.

Concealed behind a tree was someone with a vicious-looking hunting bow. An arrow had already been fitted to the string, and was now aimed directly at the boys!

CHAPTER XIV

Amazing Camouflage

WITHOUT further protest, the Hardys turned and started walking back toward the helicopter.

"Take a quick look to your left, Frank," whispered Joe. "Someone's aiming an arrow at us!"

After taking a few more steps, Frank glanced over his shoulder. At that instant the man armed with the bow and arrow darted from behind one tree to another. The boy detective's keen eye recognized his face immediately.

"Bush Barney!" Frank said softly.

The brothers reached the helicopter just as the pilot was completing his inspection.

"There's some minor damage," Mack reported, "but not bad enough to prevent us from flying if we have to. You in a hurry?"

"Yes," said Frank, "we must notify the police about two men who chased us!"

"I can't radio from here," Mack told him. "But as soon as we're airborne, there won't be any interference."

"Afterward," said Frank, "we can come down again and land somewhere out of sight of the pasture and walk back here to meet the officers."

"Suits me," said Mack. "I don't like the sound of this motor yet and I'd just as soon come down and work on it some more."

In a few minutes the whirling rotor blades were carrying the young detectives skyward. Frank asked Mack to radio Bayport tower.

"Our transmitter doesn't have enough wattage to reach that far," the pilot said. He extracted a sectional air chart from his kit and examined it. "There's an omni radio station with voice facilities much closer to us," he announced. "If we climb above these hills, we should be able to establish contact, and have them relay a message for you."

Mack tuned the radio dials to a standard aviation communication frequency, then picked up the microphone and gave his identification number and approximate position. In seconds the speaker on his receiver crackled a response. Mack handed the microphone to Frank and told him to proceed with his message.

Frank requested that word be relayed to the State Police to meet the Hardys at the pasture. He

estimated the pasture's location along the secondary road, and as a double check gave its longitude
and latitude coordinates from the air chart. Several minutes passed before a response came
through.

"The State Police," the station operator
reported, "have been notified. Several officers are
on their way to the location you indicated."

Frank asked Mack to land them close to the
pasture, but to approach the area from behind a
hill so their craft would not be seen. Mack nodded
and began a rapid descent between the hills. He
followed a valley that led them back in the general
direction of the spot where they had been forced
down. Approaching from behind a hill close to the
pasture, he maneuvered the helicopter to a soft
landing in order not to strain the already partially
damaged landing gear.

"Mack, you'd better wait for us here and guard
the copter," Frank suggested.

"Will do."

The boys carefully picked their way among the
trees and brush toward the pasture. Soon it came
in sight. Frank and Joe did not speak. They communicated by sign language, which they had prac-
ticed until they could use it to perfection.

As silently as a couple of Indians, the Hardys
edged their way to the hill situated at the end of
the pasture. They stopped for a moment and
scanned the dim shadows of the woods. Both of

them listened for unusual sounds, but neither saw nor heard anything out of the ordinary.

Frank signaled his brother, indicating that they should proceed on up the slope of the hill. Suddenly he tugged at Joe's arm and pointed directly ahead.

Joe stared before him, but could see only an unbroken mass of trees and bushes. As he stepped closer, however, the trees in the foreground gradually took on an unnatural aspect. It was difficult to tell exactly why, but there was something odd in the way the trunks and leaves reflected the light.

Approaching still closer, the Hardys were amazed to see what really confronted them. Spread across a portion of the steep slope was a huge piece of heavy canvas! Painted on its surface were trees, grass, boulders, and bits of brush. The representation was so well done that it was not detectable unless viewed from within a few feet of the canvas.

"It's fantastic camouflage!" Joe remarked, breaking their silence for the first time.

"Sure is," Frank agreed, gazing at the canvas almost in disbelief. "I'm willing to bet that behind this is the opening to a cave!"

The young sleuths traced the canvas to where it terminated at one side. Together, they carefully pulled it aside far enough to get a glimpse of what lay behind.

A huge opening was revealed. The Hardys

peered inside. Although the interior was practically in blackness, they could see that it was the entrance to a very deep cave of immense size!

Each boy took a pocket flashlight and directed the beams into the darkness. So deep was the cave, however, that the lights appeared to fade off into nothingness.

"I don't hear a sound," Frank said. "It must be empty."

"Let's take a look around!" Joe suggested, his voice tense with excitement.

"Okay!" Frank agreed. "But we'll have to let the police know where we are. I'll stay here and keep an eye on the cave. You go back to the copter, tell Mack about this place, and ask him to send the police here."

Joe started off at a sprint. Frank positioned himself behind some real brush near the camouflaged entrance. It was not long before Joe came bounding back.

"Everything's all set," he said.

The boys pushed their way around the edge of the canvas and stepped into the cave. As their eyes became accustomed to the dark interior, they could make out rough rocky surfaces curving into an arch high above their heads. The faint sound of their footsteps was amplified in a series of echoes that seemed to bounce back at them from all sides. Frank played his beam of light toward the floor.

"Look!" he said. "There are wheel grooves in

here, just like the ones we spotted on the pasture."

The Hardys followed the ruts deeper into the cave. After advancing for several yards, Joe suddenly came to a stop.

"An airplane!" he exclaimed, astounded.

Frank pointed his flashlight in the same direction. The beams picked from the darkness a sleek, multiengine plane with tricycle landing gear.

"It was taxied in here!" Joe marveled.

"From the pasture," said Frank. "The floor of this cave is about on the same level as the field, and is right in line with it. The pasture itself is too short to land on or take off from. But this cave floor serves as an extension of the runway. When a plane lands, someone on the ground merely pulls the canvas camouflage aside and—*presto*—a plane has several hundred feet more to roll on!"

Joe nodded. "And when it comes to rest, inside the cave, it's automatically hidden. Very clever. Could this plane be the same one that toppled our car?"

"I can't say for sure," his brother responded, "but there's a good chance it is."

The Hardys continued exploring the cave. A little farther on they spotted a large wooden door. It was padlocked, but they noted that the hinges were not very strong. Each boy pushed hard against a section of the wood. It began to crack, then finally gave way with a resounding smash.

Frank and Joe stepped into a room formed out of the natural rock. They were astonished to see stacks of sturdy wooden boxes piled along the walls. Stamped on the side of each was: STANWIDE MINING AND EQUIPMENT COMPANY.

"Wow!" Joe exclaimed. "There must be fifty or more of these boxes here!"

"And they may contain the stolen platinum parts!" Frank said as he played his light across the stacks. "Let's break open one of the boxes and check."

The boys placed their flashlights on the floor and positioned the beams toward one stack of boxes. They then walked over, dragged off the box on top, and set it on the floor.

"Whew!" Joe was puffing. "It sure is heavy."

"We'll need something to pry open the lid," Frank said, glancing around.

Joe noticed a rusted metal rod lying on one of the stacks. He took it and forced the end under the lid of the box. Then both boys put all their weight against it. After much exertion, they began to loosen the top.

"It's beginning to give a little," Joe said.

They had nearly accomplished their task when the sound of footsteps interrupted them. The Hardys froze.

"Hands up!" growled a gruff voice from behind them.

CHAPTER XV

Capture

THE surprised boys whirled to find themselves face to face with Bush Barney and the man they had recently encountered in the pasture.

"What are you guys doing here?" the latter snarled. "I told you to get out!" The man fingered the muzzle of his shotgun, which now was pointed at the ground.

Frank and Joe were at a loss for an excuse as to their presence in the cave. Frank realized that nothing he could say would sound believable. But anything was worth a try at this point, he thought.

"We took off in the copter," he explained nonchalantly, "but it wasn't working right so we landed again. While our pilot was checking the engine, my brother and I decided to walk around a bit. It was quite by accident that we stumbled on this cave."

Bush Barney turned on a bright electric lantern and hung it on a metal spike hammered into the stone wall of the storeroom. His expression was grim.

"I don't believe a word of it!" he snapped, glancing at his companion. "I'll bet these punks already knew about the cave. They might have even been in here before."

His confederate gripped the shotgun more tightly. To the boys' relief, he did not raise it.

"Is that right, boys?" he bellowed. "Were you ever in here before?"

"No!" Joe cried out. "As my brother told you, we discovered the cave just now—by accident!" But the Hardys could see that the two men were not convinced.

Frank tried to estimate the time that had passed since the police were notified. They should be arriving soon, he told himself. In the meantime, he and Joe must keep these men talking.

"Anchor!" said Barney, addressing his partner. "You keep 'em covered while I find some rope." He went out.

The young detectives stood helpless, churning with anger at their predicament. There was no chance for them to attempt to rush at Anchor—he was watching too closely.

Minutes later, the ex-convict Bush Barney returned to the room, carrying a large coil of rope.

He took the shotgun, then handed the rope to Anchor.

"I'll hold this while you tie 'em up," he said.

Barney motioned the boys to put their hands behind their backs, and Anchor uncoiled the rope. Suddenly the sound of approaching footsteps caused the two men to stiffen.

"Anyone in here?" shouted an authoritative voice. "We're the police!"

"Quick! Dowse that light!" Anchor growled to Barney, pointing to the electric lamp hanging from the spike. He then reached out to retrieve his shotgun from Barney.

The Hardys glanced at each other. This was their chance to act! Joe spun around, kicking the shotgun out of Anchor's hands just as it was handed over.

Frank rushed Barney. Before the ex-convict could turn out the lamp, the young sleuth sent him crashing to the floor with a perfect tackle.

Joe managed to catch Anchor in a tight head lock and tumbled across the floor with him. Barney reached for the shotgun, but Frank grasped it first and threw it a distance away. With his free arm he then swung at Barney, catching the ex-convict directly on the chin. His opponent fell back, stunned.

At that instant four state troopers rushed into the room and helped the boys drag the two men to their feet. The suspects were immediately handcuffed.

"Now how about answering a few questions?" Frank demanded.

The captured men glared at the boys malevolently.

"We don't know anything!" Barney growled.

"Who owns the airplane that's kept here in the cave?" Frank pressed.

"You won't get anything out of us!" boasted Anchor.

"Do the boxes in this room contain merchandise stolen from Stanwide?" Frank continued.

The men remained stubbornly silent. The Hardys guessed it would be a waste of time to keep on trying to elicit any information from them. So they decided to get in touch with Mr. Allen and ask him to come to the cave. The boxes would be opened in his presence with the police officers as witnesses. This might help to build an airtight case against the racketeers.

"We can reach headquarters on our car radio," said one of the troopers when Frank explained the boys' plan. "Want to come along and send the message yourself?"

"Thanks."

Leaving the others to guard the two prisoners, Frank and an officer walked to the police car, parked on the road. The trooper established contact with his headquarters and Frank described the situation to the chief. Shortly a response was received telling them that Mr. Allen had been reached and would leave at once for the cave. In order to save time, a police helicopter would bring the executive to the site.

Meanwhile, Frank and the officer returned to the cave. Barney and Anchor appeared increasingly nervous. The boys hoped they would break down and answer the Hardys' questions. They still refused to speak, however.

After what seemed like an eternity of restless waiting, the sound of a helicopter's whirling rotor blades was heard faintly in the distance. The Hardys darted from the cave and into the center of the pasture. They waved their arms vigorously as the craft passed overhead. In response, it turned into a descending spiral and the pilot set the craft down gently a few yards away from the boys. The door opened and Mr. Allen stepped out.

"You two have discovered something of great importance?" he asked eagerly.

"Yes, we have," Frank answered. "We've captured two members of the gang we think is involved in the platinum thefts, and what may be the stolen merchandise."

"Congratulations!" Mr. Allen said. "You don't waste any time when working on a case."

"Thanks," Frank replied. "But the mystery is far from being solved. There's a great deal more that we'll have to uncover."

The sleuths took the executive to the cave. "Incredible!" he commented, awe-stricken. "How did you ever manage to discover this hideout?"

"We'll fill you in on the details later," Frank said. "Right now, we'd like you to check out the contents of the wooden boxes we found here."

As they came to the plane, he stared in astonishment, but did not pause. The three hurried on to the waiting group, and the executive was introduced.

As Mr. Allen and the two boys entered the storage room, Barney and Anchor looked very uneasy. The president of Stanwide took several folded sheets of paper from his coat pocket.

"These are copies of the bills of lading of the missing shipments," he said. "I've checked off what materials made up the shortages."

The Hardys lifted the lid of the box they had been opening, and Mr. Allen read off a list of items and quantities. The contents tallied exactly with some of the missing platinum parts! Two other boxes were opened, disclosing more of the items on the list!

Frank spoke to the officers. "I'd say there's enough evidence here to arrest Barney and Anchor."

"You're right," said one of the State Police officers.

Gripping each of the handcuffed men by an

arm, two of the troopers began walking them out of the cave.

Suddenly Anchor broke his silence. "Wait a minute!" he shouted. "You can't do this! We're not the head guys in this racket!"

"Who else is in this with you?" Frank prodded. "Give us their names!"

Barney nudged Anchor with his elbow, signaling him to keep silent. "I don't know who they are," Anchor mumbled meekly.

Refusing to say any more, the two suspects were led away. Mr. Allen clapped the Hardys on their shoulders. "This has been a great job on your part, fellows." The brothers grinned.

With their help Mr. Allen checked several more boxes and found that they also contained stolen parts. Joe suggested that they load as many of them as they could aboard Mack's helicopter for transport back to Stanwide. One of the troopers offered the use of the police helicopter to aid in the operation. He also told the Hardys that several men would be assigned to stand guard over the cave.

Still amazed by the camouflaged hideout, Mr. Allen took a flashlight and scanned the surroundings. For the first time he took a close look at the airplane stored there. What he saw seemed to startle him.

"It's hard to believe!" the executive murmured. "But it is!"

"What is?" asked Frank, curious.

"This airplane!" Mr. Allen answered, playing the beam of light across its sleek lines. "This was Clint Hill's!"

"But I thought that crashed!" Joe said in amazement.

Mr. Allen beckoned the Hardys to step closer to the plane. He pointed a trembling finger at something on the side of the cowling. It appeared to be a small decal, in the shape of an eagle.

"Clint put this emblem here," the executive said. "This was his personal airplane."

The boys did not speak, noting that Mr. Allen's face expressed deep sadness. Slowly walking around the plane, he stopped at the cockpit door, opened it, then climbed inside. He sat there quietly, as if expecting the lost pilot suddenly to appear.

CHAPTER XVI

Telltale Initials

GLANCING at each other, the Hardys kept silent as Mr. Allen continued to stare sorrowfully into space. They were eager to ask him more about Clint Hill's plane, but out of respect did not disturb him. He sat quietly in the cockpit for several minutes, then finally climbed out.

"I assume the airplane was sold after Hill's accident," Frank said. "Who bought it?"

"It wasn't sold to anyone," Mr. Allen replied. "The plane was stolen soon after Clint crashed."

"Stolen!" the boys cried out.

"Yes," Mr. Allen answered. "I had almost forgotten the incident."

He went on to explain that local and government authorities had investigated the theft, but had turned up nothing.

"We finally came to the conclusion," Mr. Allen

said, "that whoever stole the plane either crashed in it, or shipped it out of the country."

"Maybe Hill's ghost stole it," Joe muttered derisively.

Then another angle occurred to the boys. If Clint Hill had survived the crash at sea and was involved in the platinum racket, had he come back to steal his own airplane for use in the thefts?

Returning to the business at hand, Frank and Joe, aided by Mr. Allen and two troopers, dragged some of the boxes from the cave and the task of loading the stolen material aboard the police helicopter was begun. When the craft was packed to capacity, its pilot quickly departed for the trip back to Stanwide.

Meanwhile, Joe had hurried off to get Mack and his helicopter. Soon the craft arrived, landing on the pasture near the cave entrance. The pilot jumped out and went into the thieves' hideout to pick up more boxes for loading. As they emerged from the cave, an eerie, disembodied sound brought them to a stop. Someone unseen was whistling "High Journey." Mr. Allen's face turned ash white.

The whistling stopped. It was followed by a ghostly sounding voice. *"You can't escape from a man you've killed!"*

"That's Clint Hill's voice!" Mr. Allen gasped. He was trembling.

"Where is it coming from?" Joe asked.

"Listen!" Frank ordered as the whistling began again. He made an effort to determine its source. Suddenly Frank, followed by his brother, broke into a fast run toward the helicopter. They reached the craft just as the whistling ceased.

"It's coming from the radio receiver!" Frank shouted in amazement.

"What's going on around here?" asked Mack, completely baffled.

"I wish we knew," Frank responded, staring at the receiver.

Mr. Allen now joined the boys and Mack. "If I wasn't so sure that it was Clint Hill's voice we heard, I'd say the whole thing is a hoax," said Mr. Allen with a grimace.

"I don't believe it's just a hoax," Frank assured him. "And now shouldn't we start loading the boxes aboard?" he suggested, hoping to take Mr. Allen's mind off Hill's ghostly message.

The work was arduous, but soon the helicopter was filled to capacity, reserving enough space so that Mr. Allen could return to Stanwide with his property. The Hardys asked Mack to pick them up later.

"While we're waiting, we'll do more sleuthing in this area."

When all the cargo was secured, Mr. Allen shook hands with the boys, thanked them again, and boarded the helicopter. The pilot started the engine and set the rotor blades at a high RPM for take-off power. The craft lifted off the ground, then headed on a course to the southeast. It quickly disappeared beyond the crest of hills.

Frank and Joe returned to the cave. Two troopers had posted themselves at the entrance. The brothers went inside to take a closer look, beaming their flashlights at every inch of the rocky interior. They found nothing of significance.

Finally Joe went to the very rear of the cavern to search.

Frank, meanwhile, walked over to the airplane and climbed into the cockpit. Looking toward the rear, he spotted a small but powerful electric hoist mounted on rails that straddled a hatch in the floor of the cabin. Several hundred feet of light cable were wound around the hoist's spindle.

"What's a device like this doing in a passenger airplane?" the young detective puzzled. "And what's it used for?"

Making a mental note of the hoist, Frank turned his attention to other areas of the cabin and cockpit. He searched through all the compartments but all he found were some air charts and an old navigational plotter.

"Whoever stole this plane made sure he left nothing around to identify him!" Frank muttered.

He extracted a fingerprint kit from his pocket and dusted the wheel, instrument panel, throttle, and other normally exposed areas for telltale prints. As he had expected, there were none; the occupants had been clever enough always to wear gloves.

Frank now bent low with his flashlight and searched underneath the seats. Suddenly he noticed a small leather object jammed between those of the pilot and copilot. He had difficulty reaching it, but finally managed to grasp the object and pull it out. A leather glove!

The young detective examined the lining of the fairly new glove. What he saw caused him to shout in excitement. Marked on the lining with indelible ink were the initials L.P.

"Lance Peterson!" Frank exclaimed, bolting out of the plane.

Excitedly he called to Joe, who came running. "What's up?"

"Look!" Frank cried, thrusting the glove toward his brother.

Joe's eyes widened as he spotted the initials. "They must stand for Lance Peterson!"

"Right! Mr. Allen should know about this as soon as possible!"

The boys hurried from the cave and told the troopers of their discovery. One of the policemen took his walkie-talkie radio out of its case, pulled the telescopic antenna from its housing, and flipped a toggle switch.

"These units can't transmit more than a mile or two," the trooper said. "But one of our patrol cars might be within range somewhere. They can get a call through to Mr. Allen."

The trooper succeeded in reaching a patrol car and transmitted the message. While awaiting a response, the boys discussed Peterson's connection with the racket.

"He must have stolen Clint's plane himself," Joe surmised.

"It sure looks that way," said Frank. "But if Peterson is using the plane to fly in the stolen loot, I wonder where he makes the pickup. It certainly couldn't be Bayport. The airplane would be recognized there at once."

A crackling sound from the trooper's walkie-talkie signaled them that a message was about to come in. The policeman put the receiver to his ear and listened intently. After a couple of minutes he put down the instrument and turned to the boys.

"Mr. Allen has just arrived back at Stanwide. He has received your message and congratulates you on the new clue. Also, he wants you to know that he checked with Bayport tower and was told that nothing new has turned up on the whereabouts of Peterson and Lieber."

"Thanks," said Joe.

He suggested to his brother that since it would be another couple of hours before the helicopter returned to pick them up, they do some investigating outside the cave.

"Good idea, Joe. Say, do you remember the small cabin I spotted when we flew around here with Randy Watson?"

Joe nodded.

"I'd like to take a look at that place for clues," Frank told him. He pointed off across the road, in the direction of the heavy woods there. "If I remember correctly, the cabin should be located about a mile from here."

The Hardys told the troopers where they were going, and said they should be back in about an hour. They started off at a fast pace.

"This sure is tough traveling," Joe remarked as they picked their way up a hillside among closely spaced trees and tangled brush.

"It's rugged," Frank agreed. "But we ought to be getting close to the cabin soon."

The boys continued to plod ahead. Finally Joe tugged at Frank's arm and pointed to a small clearing a little to his right.

"The cabin!" he whispered.

The boys proceeded cautiously and stopped at the edge of the clearing. The cabin was weatherbeaten and dilapidated.

Again Joe pointed. "Look! The door's halfway open!"

"There doesn't seem to be anyone around," Frank answered in low tones.

The boys bent down and edged their way closer. They stepped with meticulous care to avoid making any noise. Suddenly the cabin door slammed shut with a loud bang. Startled, the boys quickly dashed for cover behind a large tree and focused their eyes on the building.

CHAPTER XVII

A Revealing List

TENSE and excited, Frank and Joe watched the cabin door. Suddenly it swung open, then slammed shut again. During the next few moments this cycle was repeated several times.

"What's going on?" Joe whispered.

Frank glanced at the surrounding trees. He noticed that the leaves were moving, and grinned.

"It's the wind," he said. "The door is being blown open and shut. It must have a faulty latch."

The boys studied the cabin for a sign somebody was around. When they were fairly certain that no one was nearby, they stepped from behind the cover of the tree.

"I'm going into the cabin," Frank announced. "You stay on guard here."

"Be careful," Joe urged. "If you need help, just yell."

Frank slowly approached the cabin. The door

swung open and was about to slam shut again when the young sleuth grabbed the knob. Stealthily he poked his head inside the building.

The cabin's one small room was in deplorable condition. Unwashed dishes were piled in a metal basin, articles of clothing were scattered about, and dust lay everywhere. "Wouldn't Aunt Gertrude fuss if she could see this mess!" Frank said to himself, chuckling.

He stepped into the room and looked around for clues. At one end was a stone fireplace in which were scattered several charred logs. Flanking each side of the fireplace were numerous boat anchors of varying shapes and sizes. "This is Anchor's place, all right," thought Frank. "I can see how he got his nickname."

The young detective spotted a supply of canned foods, stacked on a wooden shelf above the sink. Realizing he was hungry, Frank opened a couple of cans of meat. He then took them outside and shared their contents with Joe.

"Anchor brand meat, eh?" Joe grinned. "Remind me to thank that crook!"

Frank returned to the cabin to continue his investigation. After a thorough search, he found nothing. Frank was about to give up when something in the fireplace caught his eye. It was a charred piece of paper. Lifting it carefully out of the ashes, he placed it gently on the floor.

Bending down, the young sleuth saw that it contained a list of names. The printing was extremely faint, but he could make out the names Peterson, Anchor, and Rodax. At the bottom of the list was a skull and crossbones and the initials C.H.

"C.H.," Frank repeated. "Could they stand for Clint Hill?"

On a hunch Frank picked up a bucket of firewood located nearby and dumped the contents on the floor. Among the wood was a crumpled fragment of paper which appeared to have been torn from a small loose-leaf diary. Frank smoothed out the paper and found written on it:

That ghost knows too much!

Excited, Frank rushed outside to show Joe his discovery. Joe examined the note, then pointed to a patch of ground near the cabin.

"I've made an interesting discovery of my own," he said, and led Frank to the spot. Impressed clearly in the earth was a set of footprints. The instep of the right foot was narrower than that of the left.

"Clint Hill's footprints again!" Frank exclaimed.

"And they appear to be quite fresh," Joe said.

Frank stared at the prints. "Now I'm convinced Clint Hill *is* alive! If he was double-crossed by the gang, maybe he's plaguing them for revenge, or to extort money from them in return for keeping quiet about their activities."

"That could be the reason why Peterson wanted

us to track down the ghost," Joe replied. "Once we found Hill, he could get rid of him."

"Possibly," Frank said. "Then again, we could have Hill all wrong. He could be working to bring the gang to justice in his own way."

Frank took an envelope from his pocket and gently inserted the charred piece of paper he had found.

"Mack should be here soon to pick us up," he said. "We'd better get back to Bayport pronto and show this new evidence to Mr. Allen."

The boys returned to the pasture. They had waited only a few minutes when they saw the helicopter skimming over the tops of the hills. The pilot descended directly over the pasture and touched down a few yards away. The boys climbed into the cabin and the craft lifted off the ground.

A brisk tail wind carried the helicopter along at a ground speed greater than that normally experienced, shortening the return flight by almost fifteen minutes. Mack set the craft down on a grass-covered area near the Ace Air Service ramp, and the Hardys hurried off to telephone Mr. Allen.

"I'll meet you at Peterson's office in a few minutes," he said.

Minutes later, the two detectives were walking through the company hangar. They noticed that all of Stanwide's aircraft were out except one. As the Hardys passed it, a man suddenly jumped from behind the plane and, unnoticed by the boys, lobbed a spherical-shaped metal object at them. It struck the concrete floor, bounded hard once, then rolled directly toward the brothers.

"Hit the floor! Quick!" Frank shouted as he recognized the object. "That's a hand grenade!"

The boys hurled themselves flat and folded their arms over their heads. A split second later they heard an ear-shattering explosion, then the piercing whine of shrapnel flying above them.

The concussion rocked the hangar. Metal fragments from the grenade tore into the wings and fuselage of the plane. The high-octane fuel gushed out of the plane's wing tanks, buckled by the blast.

Half dazed, the boys scrambled to their feet. The churning dust and smoke choked them.

"We'd better get out of here!" Joe cried out. "If that fuel catches fire, this place will go up like a torch!"

Outside the hangar, the Hardys glanced around to see if the man who had thrown the grenade was in sight, but he had vanished. A small crowd had gathered, attracted by the explosion.

An airport fire truck rolled into the hangar. Its crew quickly sprayed the plane and the floor with chemical foam to prevent the fuel from igniting.

Just then Mr. Allen arrived. "What happened here? What's all the commotion?" he asked.

"Someone tossed a grenade at us in there!" Joe answered, wiping beads of perspiration from his forehead.

"The gang we're after sure plays rough!" said Frank, angered.

Mr. Allen's face showed his apprehension. "Things are becoming too dangerous. Maybe you boys should give up the case."

"We're not quitting now!" Frank declared.

"We have the gang worried. They're desperate, and want us out of the way. This grenade business proves it."

The Hardys and Mr. Allen walked together to Peterson's office. There, Frank showed the executive the names on the paper he had discovered in the cabin.

"This ties in with some news I have for you," Mr. Allen said. "I have just learned that Rodax

has suddenly resigned his job. He told the payroll master, who was the last to see him, that he had been offered a better job with another firm."

"Did Rodax say where?" Frank queried.

"No, only that it was a long distance from here. He collected what pay was due him and disappeared."

"How about Mrs. Rodax?" Joe asked. "Has anyone questioned her yet?"

"I telephoned his home," Mr. Allen said. "Mrs. Rodax informed me that her husband left and did not say what his destination was. He told her only that he was going on a confidential trip."

"What time did Rodax leave the plant?" Frank asked.

"Late this morning, according to the payroll master."

"Then it's too late to try tailing him," Frank said, disappointed.

"Another thing," the executive said. "One of the shipping-room clerks, John Unger, also quit his job suddenly."

Frank remarked, "He too could be working with the gang."

Joe stood nearby in deep thought. "I have a hunch," he said. "It's pretty obvious they never did reach California, and no word has been received of their landing anywhere else in this country—or Canada or Mexico."

"Where *do* you think they are?" Mr. Allen asked with interest.

"Ile de la Mer," Joe answered. "Since it's uninhabited, it would make a great hideout—and Peterson would remember the air route from the trip he and Clint Hill were making when their plane crashed at sea."

Both Frank and the company president were impressed by Joe's theory.

"It's worth looking into!" Frank exclaimed, and turned to Mr. Allen. "Could you arrange for Joe and me to go there?"

"I certainly can," Mr. Allen said. "But not without protection. I'm going to assign a husky body guard to accompany you!"

CHAPTER XVIII

Air-Chart Secret

ELATED at the prospect of the trip, the brothers hurried home to discuss the island hop with Mr. Hardy. The ace detective was apprehensive, especially after hearing about the grenade incident. He agreed, however, that a search of Ile de la Mer would certainly be worthwhile.

"I'd like to make the trip with you," their father said. "But there are too many loose ends in the case to be taken care of here." His expression became grave. "Be on your guard," he warned his sons. "This is a clever gang we're up against."

The Hardys were just finishing dinner when Mr. Allen telephoned. "I've obtained the use of a twin-engine amphibian aircraft to take you boys to Ile de la Mer. Jerry Madden will be your pilot," the executive announced. "I've also managed to get two big, strapping fellows from the plant to go along."

"Great," Frank answered. "And thanks. We'll need only a day to get ready."

"Keep me posted on developments," said Mr. Allen, "and good luck!"

Only a few minutes passed before the telephone rang again.

"Hello?" said Frank.

"This is the ghost of Clint Hill," an eerie voice announced. *"I warn you, dead men tell no tales."*

Frank gripped the phone tighter. "Who *is* this?"

There was a moment of silence, then a loud burst of laughter.

"Chet!" Frank exclaimed. "You had me fooled."

"You're speaking to a master impersonator," Chet boasted.

Suddenly Frank was struck with an idea. "Listen, pal, your ghost imitation may come in handy. How'd you like to fly down to Ile de la Mer with Joe and me?"

"Count me in!" Chet responded excitedly. "Just make sure there's enough food aboard!"

The next day the brothers went to the Morton farmhouse to give Chet more details concerning the trip. They found Iola Morton, Chet's pretty, dark-haired sister, and Callie Shaw, an attractive blonde, seated in the living room. Callie was Frank's favorite date, while Joe liked Iola very

much. Standing in the middle of the room was
Chet. He was whistling "High Journey."

"Hi, fellows!" he called, interrupting his per-
formance long enough to take several bites out of
the massive sandwich he was holding.

"Hi!" Frank and Joe grinned as they took seats
near the two girls.

"As you can see," Iola said with a smile, "Chet is
probably one of the best-fed ghosts in the business."

"I need all the energy I can get," Chet defended
himself. "I might even start my own ghost-to-ghost
network!"

By this time he had finished his sandwich, and
hurried to the kitchen. Seconds later, he reappeared holding a large roasted turkey leg. Using it
as a baton to mark the tempo, he resumed whistling.

"What if the real ghost gets mad at you for
imitating him and decides to haunt you?" said Joe,
chuckling.

Chet stopped whistling. He paled slightly. "Uh,
come on, fellows," he quavered. "You don't think
Clint Hill is a real ghost, do you?"

"We can't say for sure," Frank answered, trying
to act solemn. "After all, we've never seen him.
We've only heard him speak."

Chet suddenly found his turkey leg unappetiz-
ing. He laid it down on a plate. The girls began
giggling.

"This is no laughing matter," he said with a frown. But suddenly his expression brightened. "I know what I'll do if Hill is a ghost! If he tries to scare us, I'll scare him right back!"

Chet dashed from the room. Moments later he reappeared, his stout form draped in a white sheet. The others roared with laughter as Chet leaped playfully about the room with the sheet swirling behind him.

"Better watch where you're going!" Frank warned the cavorting phantom.

Chet now spread his arms wide under the sheet. Looking like a huge white bat, he took a high running jump across the room. Coming down hard, he tripped on one corner of the sheet. Chet lost his balance, stumbled, then fell and rolled across the room in a tangled mass of cloth. The girls joined in the Hardys' fresh outburst of laughter.

"What's so funny?" Chet groaned as he struggled to free himself. "I thought I looked pretty scary."

"If Hill's ghost ever saw you in that get-up," Frank said, "he'd laugh so hard he wouldn't be able to haunt anyone."

Chet finally extricated himself and plunked down into a chair with a disgruntled expression. Just then Mrs. Morton appeared and invited everyone to have lunch. As they all ate, the three boys discussed the trip to Ile de la Mer.

"Wish I were going," Iola said wistfully.

A little later Chet accompanied the Hardys to the airport so they might check the plans for the trip. As they approached the Stanwide hangar, the boys spotted a twin-engine amphibian aircraft parked on the macadam ramp in front of the building. As they walked up to the craft, Jerry Madden's head suddenly popped from a window in the cockpit.

"Hello, fellows!" he called. "How do you like her?"

"A beauty!" Joe responded as they all admired the craft's graceful lines and bright painted surfaces.

Jerry's head vanished into the cockpit. A moment later a door opened in the side of the fuselage and he reappeared.

"We just finished installing the long-range tanks," Jerry announced. "As it stands now, we can make Ile de la Mer nonstop and still have a couple of hours' fuel in reserve."

"What about the return flight?" Frank asked. "Won't we have to refuel?"

"According to Mr. Allen," Jerry explained, "the exploratory team he sent to the island took a sizable supply of aviation gasoline with them. It was stored in 55-gallon drums. Some of them may have been unloaded and might still be there. However, if we find it's gone—or is unusable—the company will have more fuel flown down to us."

After finding that everything was in readiness, Frank said he thought they should plan to depart as soon as practicable. "Tonight, maybe?"

"Okay!" Jerry replied. "I'll give the plane a final check, then see what the weather bureau will give us in the way of a route forecast. It would be good to leave tonight. Then we'd arrive at the island after sunrise tomorrow."

The boys hurried off to make final preparations. The Hardys dropped Chet at his house, telling him they would return within a couple of hours. After arriving at their own house, Frank and Joe learned that their father had gone out of town.

Mrs. Hardy and Aunt Gertrude began preparing a substantial supper for the boys while they packed some light luggage. The two women tried hard to conceal their apprehension, but it showed on their faces. The boys assured them everything would be all right.

Finally they departed for the airport, picking up Chet on the way. As they walked toward the Stanwide hangar, the boys spotted Jerry Madden standing near the airplane. There were two men with him—tall, muscular fellows who appeared to be in their late twenties. The pilot introduced them as Bill Vogel and Kurt Lerner, the men Mr. Allen had selected to go on the trip. Bill and Kurt greeted the boys with hard, firm handshakes.

"Wow!" Chet whispered as he straightened out the fingers of his right hand. "I'm glad those two are on *our* side."

Soon everyone was aboard the amphibian and the engines were started.

"How is the weather forecast?" Frank asked Jerry as they waited for the motors to warm up.

"Excellent!" Jerry replied. "However, there is a strong low-pressure system situated southwest of Ile de la Mer. It could develop into quite a storm center. Right now, it's hard to say in just what direction it may move. But at present it shouldn't give us any trouble."

He told the boys that once out of the continental United States, he would have to ask for Defense Visual Flight Regulation. After scanning the instrument panel methodically, Jerry picked up the microphone and communicated with Bayport tower. He asked for taxi and take-off instructions, and requested that his DVFR flight plane be activated.

Upon lining up the craft on the active runway to which he was cleared, Jerry eased the throttles ahead to maximum power. After a short run, the plane lifted off the ground easily. Jerry pulled up a small lever, which retracted the wheels into the fuselage.

When he reached the selected cruising altitude, Jerry set the plane on course. Hour after hour passed as it bore through the sky. Lulled by the drone of the engines, the boys caught up on some sleep.

When they awoke, the first light of dawn was breaking in the east. Gradually the light grew brighter, revealing a fascinating mosaic of deep blue and jade green on the surface of the ocean below.

"How long have we been flying over water?" Frank asked.

"Quite some time," Jerry replied. "We left the United States coast about three hours ago."

"You must be tired," Frank said.

"Not really," Jerry responded. "I slept most of yesterday. Also, the automatic pilot gives me a chance to stretch my arms and legs once in a while."

Chet had wasted no time looking into the food supplies for breakfast. The meal, consisting mostly of fresh fruit, was divided among the group.

"We must be getting close to Ile de la Mer," Jerry told the boys. He examined his chart closely. "Of course I'm basing that on dead reckoning, which is not always as precise as we would like it to be. But do you see those cumulus clouds ahead?"

The boys nodded.

"Clouds like that generally form over patches of land, such as an island," Jerry said.

He maintained his course. Gradually the irregular outline of a small island loomed on the horizon.

"That's Ile de la Mer!" Jerry exclaimed. "I've seen aerial shots of it that Clint Hill sent to Mr. Allen. It has a particular wedgelike shape which is unmistakable!"

He eased the nose of the plane down and descended to a lower altitude. Then Jerry aimed at the island and approached it at treetop height. Zooming in over the rocky coast, he pulled the nose of the plane sharply upward and followed the contour of the hills inland.

"There doesn't appear to be any level terrain to land on," he observed.

"Nothing suitable along the coast?" Frank asked.

"Much too rocky!" Jerry responded. "We'll have to make a water landing."

The pilot searched the coastline for a cove or inlet that would shelter the plane from the rougher waters of the open sea. Finally he spotted a small cove on the south side of the island.

Carefully studying the surface conditions, Jerry approached the cove and flared out several feet above the water. He now eased the throttles back and let the hull of the plane settle into the water. Taxiing into the cove, he called for the anchors to be heaved, then shut off the engines.

"The island looks deserted," Joe commented.

"Just the same we had better be careful," Frank warned. "Members of the gang could be in hiding somewhere."

Jerry assured himself that the aircraft was secured firmly, then he inflated a large rubber raft to take the group to shore.

"I'm sure I can find the old campsite of the exploratory team," Jerry said. "Mr. Allen described it to me in detail."

The Hardys, Chet, Kurt Lerner, and Bill Vogel followed the pilot through the thick trees and brush. Luckily it was not long before the group broke out into a clearing. There they found a small wooden shack, various pieces of machinery, and a number of 55-gallon drums marked "Aviation Gasoline."

Chet and Jerry examined the fuel supply, while the Hardys, accompanied by Bill and Kurt, went into the shack. They found it to be in good condition, and cans of food were stored on shelves along one wall.

"By the looks of things here," Frank observed, "I'd say this place has been occupied recently."

The boys scrutinized the interior closely for clues to the occupant but saw nothing unusual. Then Joe noticed something white sticking out behind a row of cans on the top shelf. He reached up and pulled down two large folded sheets of paper. As he unfolded them, his eyes widened with excitement.

"Frank!" he exclaimed. "Take a look at this!"

Joe pointed to his discovery. "Planning charts for aerial navigation! And here are course lines drawn on them!"

Frank dashed outside to summon Jerry and Chet. The pilot examined the charts with avid interest.

"The course lines start at the exact latitude and longitude of this island," Jerry declared.

He traced the line with his finger. It ran off the first chart, and continued on the second. The course led back into the United States to the approximate location of the camouflaged cave the Hardys had discovered. From there, it went to a point in a sparsely settled region of Montana.

"How do you figure this mystery?" Jerry asked.

Frank answered. "The gang must have been operating between the cave and this island. After we discovered the cave and things got hot for them, they decided to establish a new hideout in Montana."

"Let's go there!" Joe exclaimed.

Even Chet was enthusiastic about the idea. "Maybe I'll still get a chance to play ghost!"

"Can the plane make it to Montana nonstop?" Joe questioned.

"With full fuel tanks, and favorable winds, we

can make it at least most of the way," the pilot replied. "We may have to stop once to refuel."

Suddenly they all became aware that a strong wind was building up. Jerry ran out of the shack and scanned the sky. A dark, threatening layer of clouds was moving toward the island.

"That storm center I told you about!" he shouted to the others. "It has started moving—and it's coming right across this place!"

The storm now seemed to be approaching with increasing speed. The winds grew stronger, and intermittent droplets of rain began to pelt the area.

"Quick!" Jerry ordered. "Let's get back to the plane! Those anchors won't hold in a big storm!"

Followed by the Hardys, Chet, and the two Stanwide men, he ran off into the brush and back along the path over which they had come.

The wind became more violent and the rain was falling steadily. It quickly increased to a heavy downpour which stung the faces of the boys and their companions.

Reaching the cove, the group leaped into the raft and started paddling toward the plane, which was already being tossed around like a cork. Despite all their efforts, progress was slow. Each stroke of the paddles took the raft only a few inches ahead.

Finally, they managed to reach the plane. Jumping onto it from the raft was a precarious operation. The craft rolled and pitched violently under the pounding of the waves.

The Hardys glanced at the anchor ropes anxiously. They were being strained taut.

"Those ropes will snap any minute!" Frank thought fearfully.

CHAPTER XIX

Hideout Trap

THE storm had now become a raging fury. Huge waves crashed against the hull of the amphibian, causing it to heave violently.

"Those anchor ropes aren't going to hold!" Jerry yelled.

"What about putting out more lines?" suggested Frank.

"We have extra rope aboard," said the pilot, "but what do we attach it to? We haven't any more anchors."

"I can carry the other ends of the ropes to shore in the raft and tie them to the rocks," Frank replied.

"Too dangerous!" Jerry shouted above the wind. "The raft would be swamped in a sea like this!"

"We have no choice," Frank answered. "We'll have to take the chance."

Frank worked his way aft and picked up two coils of rope. Joe and the others pitched in to help. Climbing outside and clinging to the heaving fuselage, they fastened one end of a coil of rope to the tail, the end of the other to the bow.

Carrying both coils with him, Frank jumped into the raft and began paddling toward shore, feeding out lengths of rope behind him. The raft pitched violently in all directions. Then suddenly a towering wave crashed over the young detective. The paddle was yanked from his hand and the raft turned over.

"Frank! *Frank!*" shouted Joe.

Suddenly his brother's head bobbed up in the tossing sea. He still clung to one of the ropes. Joe and the others grabbed it at their end and began hauling him in. As Frank neared the hull, another wave hit and slammed him against the plane. Although dazed by the blow, he continued to cling to the rope. Finally he was hauled aboard. They all climbed back inside the airplane.

"Good try, Frank!" said Kurt Lerner.

"Too bad I got swamped."

"What'll we do now?" Joe asked as he felt the plane lurch hard against the anchor ropes.

"I have an idea!" said Jerry. "It's our last chance!"

Scrambling forward, he strapped himself into the pilot's seat. There he pumped the throttles a few times, worked the fuel primers, and turned on the engine ignition switches.

"What are you going to do?" Frank asked.

"Try to meet the storm on its own terms!" Jerry said grimly. "If we can get started, I can head into the wind and try to ride it out!"

He engaged the engine starters. The propellers turned slowly, but the engines failed to respond.

At that instant a series of massive waves spilled over the plane. The craft heaved violently, snapping first one anchor rope, then the other. The plane began to drift rapidly toward the jagged rocks on shore.

Jerry continued to work the starters, but the engines would not respond! "The ignition harnesses must be wet!" the pilot's voice held a note of helplessness.

Chet looked out. The rocks were getting closer! "We'll be smashed to pieces!" he yelled, taking a deep breath.

Frank rushed forward and climbed into the seat beside Jerry's. Frantically he tried to help with the starting procedure.

"We'd better get ready to jump overboard!" Jerry declared as he glanced at the deadly rocks looming up in front of his window.

Frank and Jerry continued to work the throttles and engage the starters. Suddenly the right engine backfired a few times, then burst into life.

Using the one engine, Jerry swung the plane around and headed into the wind and oncoming waves. By applying full power, he was able to halt the craft's drift toward the rocks.

"That was close!" Frank said, sighing in relief.

"We're not out of this yet," Jerry said. "With only one engine running, we have to apply so much power to hold our position that we're likely to burn out the motor!"

He again tried starting the left engine. Finally his persistence paid off. The engine backfired once, then roared in response.

Jerry eased the throttles ahead and pulled still farther away from the rocks. He reduced power sufficiently to hold their position, yet prevent the engines from overheating.

"Great job!" said Frank, and Jerry gave a wry smile.

The waves continued to batter the plane. Water seeped in through seams around the windows and the door, making it necessary for the occupants to bail constantly.

"How can the plane take this pounding?" Frank asked.

"It's a strong ship," Jerry answered. "Also, the fact that we're in a cove is helping to take some of the kick out of the waves."

The wind and the rain continued to rage. Jerry glanced at the fuel gauges.

"If this storm doesn't end soon," he observed gloomily, "we'll run out of fuel. Then we'll really be in trouble!"

Gradually, however, the rain and gusts of wind seemed to diminish in activity.

"I think the storm is moving off!" Joe said happily.

"You're right," Jerry agreed.

As night fell, the rain stopped and the wind subsided to a gentle breeze. Switching on the plane's bright landing lights, the pilot carefully taxied to a narrow part of the cove. Retrieving the rope which they had attached to the bow of the plane, Frank and Joe swam ashore and tied the end around a rock. Meanwhile, Lerner and Vogel had tied the stern line to another rock at the opposite side of the cove.

Satisfied that the airplane was now secure, the whole group fell exhausted on the beach and slept soundly through the remainder of the night.

The next day, after a breakfast from the plane's store of provisions, Jerry began an examination of the craft for damage. The Hardys, with Chet, Lerner, and Vogel, set out to collect the drums of aviation gasoline. It was long, arduous work. Each of the drums had to be rolled through the brush to the shore of the cove, loaded onto the raft, which had washed ashore undamaged, then ferried to the plane. There the contents were emptied into the fuel tanks.

It was late afternoon before the refueling operation was completed. The boys then made a quick tour of the small island, but found no one hiding there. Jerry, meanwhile, had examined every inch of the plane and reported it to be airworthy.

"I suggest we take off immediately, while we still have some daylight," he said.

Soon they were airborne again, headed for Montana. They flew throughout the night. Shortly after daybreak, Jerry landed once to refuel, then set off again. By late morning he announced that they were over Montana.

"I'll head for the area indicated on that chart you boys found on the island," said the pilot.

When they reached it, he established a search pattern by maneuvering the aircraft into a series of weaving courses. The boys looked with fascination at the twisting valleys and rivers below. Mountains jutted up all around them.

"Exactly what is it we're looking for?" Chet questioned.

"The gang's hideout would have to be near a long, level stretch of ground which could serve as a runway," Frank answered. "This particular area is rugged, so there can't be too many spots for landing."

Jerry applied more power and climbed to a higher altitude to clear some of the lower mountains. He continued the search pattern.

"It's like looking for a needle in a haystack," Chet mumbled.

"Wait a minute," said Frank. "Let's take a closer look at that spot over there." He pointed slightly to his right.

Jerry rolled into a turn and straightened out in the direction Frank had indicated.

"See the timber line on the side of that mountain ahead?" Frank asked. "There's a stretch of level ground right above it."

"I see it!" Joe exclaimed. "And say, there's a shack in a clearing in those woods about half a mile away."

The pilot also sighted the spot. He maneuvered the plane closer to the level area.

"What do you think?" Frank asked Jerry.

"It's level enough and plenty long for a landing. I'd say it would make an ideal runway. And that grove of trees at the far end would be a perfect hiding place for an airplane."

Frank suggested that they land and investigate the area. Jerry headed the plane down and flew at a height of less than a hundred feet above the ground.

"The surface looks smooth," he said. "I'm going to swing around and make a long approach for a landing."

He rolled the plane into a turn and then lined it up with the level stretch of ground, reduced power, extended the landing gear, and lowered full flaps. The craft touched down smoothly and rolled to a stop with plenty of room to spare. Jerry taxied toward the grove of trees, shut off the engines, and parked. The Hardys, followed by the others, got out and glanced around at the hard, bare ground.

"It doesn't look as if anyone has been here before," Frank remarked glumly.

"I guess we're just on a wild-goose chase," Joe said with a frown.

"Hey, fellows!" yelled Chet, who had been reconnoitering an area that sloped away from the grove of trees where the ground was softer.

Frank and Joe rushed over to their chum.

"Look!" Chet said, pointing at the ground. "Footprints!"

All the boys examined the tracks closely. The heavy impressions of a man's shoes were clear, and led down the slope. "The prints were made recently!" Joe concluded.

Excitedly the young detectives followed the trail of prints. Lerner and Vogel tagged along a short distance behind. Jerry Madden remained with the plane.

Suddenly Frank stopped and gazed straight ahead. He gestured for everyone to be quiet. Through the trees they could see a small shack.

Motioning Joe to follow him, Frank began to creep toward it. Reaching the shack, the boys peered through a knothole in the wall. What they saw startled them. Seated inside were Lance Peterson and Aaron Lieber! Tensely the Hardys each pressed an ear to the wall in hopes of overhearing the men's conversation.

"Why should we divide the loot equally?" the boys heard Lieber growl. "We did most of the work."

"We'll only divvy up what we've already unpacked," Peterson replied. "The stuff we buried in the old dry well won't be missed by the others. We'll keep that for ourselves."

"The rest of the guys ought to be flying in soon," Lieber said.

This remark startled and worried the boys. They must hurry to capture these men before the new arrivals might capture the Hardys and their companions!

When the brothers reported what they had heard, Lerner and Vogel offered to rush the place and seize Peterson and Lieber.

Frank did not agree. "They may be armed," he said. "By the time we broke into the shack, they'd have a chance to use their weapons. Let's get them to come outside."

"How?" Joe asked.

Frank grinned at his brother, then turned to Chet. "Here's your chance to play ghost."

Chet and the Hardys hid behind some brush located a short distance from the shack. Vogel and Lerner took up concealed positions nearby.

"Okay." Frank quickly whispered something to his stout friend. "You're on."

Chet cleared his throat, then called out in deep, eerie tones:

"This is the ghost of Clint Hill! You cannot escape a man that you have killed!"

A second later Peterson and Lieber bolted from the shack. Terror-stricken, they looked around.

"The ghost! It's the ghost!" Peterson screamed. "We've got to get away!"

Lerner and Vogel sprang out from a bush. Leaping on the two thieves, they quickly overpowered them.

"What—what's going on?" Lieber shouted, dumfounded.

The captured men were even more startled to see the Hardys striding toward them.

"What are you two doing here?" Lieber yelled.

"How did you find us?" blurted Peterson. "And where's the ghost?"

"Never mind," said Frank. "Who else is in the gang with you?"

"We're not talking," growled Lieber.

"If you won't tell us, we'll find out anyway," said Frank. "Bush Barney and Anchor are in jail. We know some more of your pals are due here shortly."

The prisoners glanced at each other apprehensively. They were herded into the shack, seated in chairs, and their hands tied firmly behind their backs.

Frank said that he and Joe would guard the two captives. He instructed Lerner, Vogel, and Chet to go back and warn Jerry that more members of the gang were flying in.

"Make sure our own plane is hidden," Frank commanded. "Then wait there and nab whoever arrives."

Alone with Peterson and his henchman, the Hardys began to question them. Peterson offered to make a deal, but the boys refused to listen. The only concession Frank would make was that it might go easier for the men if they would cooperate.

That seemed to make up Peterson's mind. "I can give you a complete list of everybody who's in this with us," he said, "and how the whole operation worked. You'll find it all in that metal box up there on the top shelf." He nodded toward the opposite end of the room.

Frank walked over to the shelf Peterson had indicated. He looked up at the box. It was not very large, but difficult to reach.

"I'll give you a hand," Joe said, coming over.

They stepped closer and began lifting the box. The next instant there was a click, and suddenly the floor beneath their feet gave way! A trap door! The boys plunged helplessly into a dark hole.

Landing with a thud on soft ground some ten feet below, the Hardys scrambled up just as the door slammed shut above them. At once they became aware of a hissing sound in the darkness.

"What's that odor?" Joe asked frantically.

"It must be some kind of gas, Joe!"

In the room above they heard the two men break into raucous laughter. As the hissing sound continued, the boys realized with horror that they were losing consciousness!

CHAPTER XX

Runway Victory

MEANWHILE, Chet and the two men had arrived back at the plane. Jerry was amazed to hear that Peterson and Lieber had been captured.

"And more members of the gang are expected to land here at any time," Chet added. "Frank says to hide the plane."

"We'd better push it under the trees," Jerry said.

Together, they rolled the aircraft deep into the little grove. Then they watched the sky and waited.

"I hope there aren't too many of them," Chet said nervously.

Nearly an hour passed before the droning sound of an airplane was heard in the distance.

"There it is!" Jerry shouted. "Let's take cover!"

They watched the craft as it circled and headed in for a landing. The pilot set the plane down gently, then taxied toward the grove. The plane came to a stop and three men climbed out.

"One of those men is Rodax," Vogel whispered. "He worked at the Stanwide plant."

"And I've seen the short guy around the plant too," added Lerner. "Name's Unger—he's one of the shipping clerks."

Neither he nor Vogel recognized the third man, who had piloted the plane.

"I don't recognize him, either," said Jerry.

The three men started walking toward the trees. When they sighted the amphibian, they came to an abrupt stop.

"I didn't know we had another plane working with us," Rodax was heard to say.

The men walked forward for a closer look.

"Let's get them!" Chet whispered.

He and the others leaped on the thieves. Rodax and his companions were caught completely unawares. They were quickly subdued, almost without a struggle.

"What is this?" bellowed Rodax.

At that instant Chet had an idea. He realized that Rodax and the other two henchmen had never seen him before. However, they did recognize Jerry Madden, Lerner, and Vogel as employees of Stanwide. Perhaps if the thieves were led to believe that Peterson and Lieber had talked them into coming in on the deal without their confederates' knowledge, it might make Rodax and the others angry enough to talk.

"You might call it a double cross!" Chet said.

"Double cross? What do you mean?" Rodax demanded.

The man Lerner had recognized as the shipping clerk appeared greatly alarmed.

"Maybe Peterson has brought these guys in on the deal," he said, "and plans to push us out!"

"Is that right?" Rodax shouted angrily.

"Why don't you ask Peterson and Lieber about that?" Chet taunted with a grin. "Ask them about the little—er—agreement we made with them."

Jerry and the others quickly caught on to what Chet was trying to do, and played along.

"If those guys did double-cross us, it'll be just too bad for them!" shouted Rodax. He was now in a furious mood.

The three thieves were marched off to the shack. As they approached, Peterson and Lieber, who had freed themselves from their bonds, came running out the door.

"It must be true!" growled Rodax. He leaped toward Peterson with clenched fists and knocked him to the ground. The shipping clerk rushed at Lieber. The pilot did not attempt to join in, but merely stood watching nervously.

"Let them fight it out among themselves!" yelled Chet. Concerned about the Hardys, he ran into the shack. "Frank!" he called in a worried voice. "Joe!"

Chet rushed outside.

"Jerry!" he cried out. "Frank and Joe are gone!"

Exhausted from their violent struggle, the four thieves painfully got to their feet.

"What has happened to the Hardys?" Chet demanded angrily.

Peterson and Lieber remained silent.

"Let's tie them up!" said Jerry.

Peterson and the others were taken into the shack, firmly bound and seated in chairs.

Chet searched the room. He was in a frenzy.

"You'd better tell us where the Hardys are," Jerry said angrily, addressing Peterson and Lieber. "Otherwise—"

Still the men refused to speak. The strange pilot, who had been getting more nervous by the minute, finally broke down.

"I was dragged into this racket!" he yelled. "I don't want to go to jail! I'll turn state's evidence!"

"What's your name?" Chet asked him.

"Kyle Rodney," he responded. "And I've been in this shack before. They have a trap door in the floor, over by those wood shelves, with a special catch that automatically releases when anyone steps on the door. Lieber designed it that way, in case snoopers did come here. Before stepping on it himself, he locked it. Your friends are probably down below."

"Shut up!" growled Lieber.

Chet, with the aid of Lerner and Vogel, pushed hard on the trap door. It swung downward. "I smell gas!" Chet exclaimed.

"It's harmless," Lieber said. "When the trap door opens, it uncorks a bottle rigged to the underside."

Chet peered into the hole. "There they are!" he shouted. "They're unconscious!"

"Only asleep," Peterson put in. "That gas wouldn't hurt anybody."

Chet grabbed a length of rope, handed one end of it to Lerner and Vogel, then lowered himself to where Frank and Joe were lying. He quickly looped the rope under Frank's arms, and called to the men to haul the young sleuth up. Then it was Joe's turn.

The boys were carried outside the shack. After several minutes in the fresh air, the Hardys began to regain consciousness.

"What happened?" Frank murmured in a weak voice.

"You and Joe fell through a trap door in the shack," explained Chet. "Some kind of gas was released that knocked you both out."

"Oh, yes, I remember now," Frank said, holding his head. Then he sat bolt upright. "How's Joe?" he asked.

"Okay," Chet assured him. "He's just a little groggy. Lucky that gas wasn't deadly!"

Within a few more minutes the boys had fully recovered. They went into the shack and questioned their prisoners.

"Why did you steal Clint Hill's airplane—the one we found in the cave?" Frank asked.

The captured men glared at the young sleuth in silence.

Frank decided to play a hunch. "That hoist in the plane—you used it to transfer the stolen goods while in flight, didn't you?" Slyly he played on Peterson's vanity. "I have to hand it to you. That was some trick! How did you manage it?"

"It was simple! I got the idea after watching some newsreel films on air-to-air refueling," Peterson boasted. Too late, he realized that he had been tricked into confessing. With nothing further to lose, he began to spell out the details of the scheme, as if wanting the boys and their friends to admire his cleverness.

"I stole Hill's plane to use in the operation, and we rigged a hoist to it. When we planned a job, I'd arrange to fly the shipment at night so we wouldn't be seen. Then Kyle Rodney, in the hoist plane, would rendezvous with me over some predetermined point, lower a light cable, and we'd transfer a few boxes of platinum parts from the Stanwide plane to his."

"I had to do it!" exclaimed Rodney. "Peterson found out that I had once been in trouble with the law and served a prison term. I was afraid I'd lose my pilot's license!"

"Your hoisting operation was pretty risky, wasn't it?" Jerry asked.

"It was the only way," Peterson confessed. "If I had had to land the cargo plane to unload the stuff, the delay would have shown up on my flight plan. That would have been a dead giveaway."

Lieber stared at Peterson. He was flushed with anger at his partner's betrayal.

"After the air-to-air heist," continued Peterson, ignoring him, "Rodney would fly the stuff to our cave hideout. Bush Barney and Anchor would then set up a roadblock to prevent motorists from using the road near the cave, for fear they might see the plane land in the pasture. If a motorist ignored the roadblock, they would set off flares to warn Rodney not to come in."

"So it was you who hit our car with the wheels of your plane the night we drove along the road!" Frank said accusingly to Rodney.

"That was an accident," Rodney answered. "Bush Barney was late in lighting the flare, and I was too low to pull up and go around."

Peterson then asked the Hardys a question. "How did you learn about this hideout?"

"That was easy," Frank replied. "We found an

air chart on Ile de la Mer with a course to this place marked on it."

"You fool!" Lieber bellowed at Peterson. "Why did you have to forget that chart!"

"What were you doing on Ile de la Mer?" Frank asked Peterson. "Did you hide any loot there?"

"No," Peterson responded. "We had planned to use it as a hideout. But then we changed our minds—we were afraid Mr. Allen might decide to send another exploratory team there."

"Bunglers!" mumbled Rodax.

"Then I remembered this spot," Peterson continued. "My grandfather used to bring me hunting here when I was a kid. I thought it would make a perfect hideout. We high-tailed it from Ile de la Mer so fast that I forgot to take the chart I had plotted the flight on."

"Who threw the hand grenade at us?" asked Joe angrily, remembering their close call in the Stanwide hangar.

"That was Rodax," Peterson said quickly, eager to disclaim responsibility for the brutal attack. "And it was his idea to get you boys to my office so he could have Lieber steal your camera and films from the plane. You'll find the camera in a Bayport pawnshop."

"Shut up!" shouted Rodax.

Joe, taking a guess, said, "Zimm, too, worked with you. He spied on us, and covered Clint Hill's prints in the hangar in case he was still alive and we might trace him. Also, Zimm tried to drop that hunk of machinery on us in the warehouse."

"Yes," Peterson replied.

Frank turned to Lieber. "Your brother-in-law is innocent, isn't he? You just used him for a dupe?"

"Yes."

The Hardys asked Peterson the location of the dry well where he and Lieber had hidden the loot that they intended keeping for themselves. On hearing this bit of treachery, Rodax and the shipping clerk were ready to tear Peterson and Lieber apart.

Frank whispered to Jerry Madden that he should summon the State Police on the plane's radio, and also request them to relay word to Bayport Police Headquarters to have Zimm arrested. The pilot left the shack. A few minutes later he returned and nodded to the young sleuth that he had been successful.

Before long, a large Montana police helicopter arrived and the thieves were taken into custody. As Peterson left, he stopped for an instant and turned to the boys.

"Remember," he said threateningly, "Clint Hill's ghost is still on the loose! You never solved that mystery!"

"No, but we mean to learn the truth," Frank

answered, and added, "You left a note to Lieber in that cabin saying the ghost knew too much, didn't you?"

"Yes, I got a lot of radio messages that were—er—too revealing. They came over my office set that was always tuned to unicom." Peterson would not explain any further.

When the Hardys and their friends returned to Bayport, they received a joyous homecoming. Mr. Allen was overwhelmed by the sleuthing ability of the boy detectives. Frank and Joe refused to accept the handsome check he offered them, but said that their friend Chet would settle for the biggest meal he could find in Bayport!

Two days later the brothers received a telephone call from Mr. Allen, asking them to come to his office. When they arrived, his secretary looked at them with a big smile.

"Go right in," she said.

As the boys opened the door to Mr. Allen's office, they were astounded to hear someone whistling "High Journey"!

"Come in!" said Mr. Allen as he rose from behind his desk. He nodded toward a bearded young man at the end of the room. "Meet Clint Hill, boys!"

The Hardys stood speechless for a moment, unable to believe their ears. Clint Hill shook hands with them, then after they all sat down, he began to relate his story.

"As you know, Peterson and I and our passengers crashed at sea during a return flight from Ile de la Mer. After we hit the water, the three mineralogists drowned almost instantly. Peterson took the one available life raft and left me clinging to the wing of the plane. I was slightly injured and couldn't swim after him."

"What did Peterson hope to gain by abandoning you?" Frank asked curiously.

"As he paddled off in the raft, he shouted to me that now he would become chief pilot of Stanwide. And that he would fix Mr. Allen. Then I fainted. I must have unconsciously clung to a piece of wreckage, because the next thing I knew I was on an island, being cared for by some natives. They spoke only their own language, which I couldn't understand."

"Lucky the natives were friendly," Frank said.

"Oh, yes," Clint replied. "After I recovered, they took me to another, bigger island in a dugout canoe. It was there that I managed to get a job and earn enough money to buy boat passage back to the United States. I decided to keep my identity a secret and stay in hiding until I found out what Peterson was up to. I didn't even get in touch with Mr. Allen—I wanted to be sure of my ground before making any accusations."

"When did you decide to become a ghost?" asked Joe, grinning.

"I knew Peterson was superstitious," the pilot said, "so I got a job with the ground crew at a field near Bayport. I began to bug him with the ghost business, hoping to make him confess not only that he had left me to die, but what he was doing to 'fix' Mr. Allen."

"Great idea!" Frank said with a chuckle. "It even had us worried for a while. I guess Peterson asked us to work for him to throw us off the track. By the way, was it you who wore a mask one night at Zimm's house and gave me a punch?"

"Was that you?" Hill asked, embarrassed. "I'm sorry. I thought it was one of Peterson's pals!"

"No harm done." Frank grinned. "Go on with your story."

"After I'd been here a while," Clint continued, "I took the airport operator I was working for into my confidence. He allowed me the use of an airplane to do some investigating, and I succeeded in tracking Peterson to Anchor's cabin, but I couldn't find the cave. I see you boys did, though! And when he skipped, I phoned your house to find out where he'd gone. But you tried to bargain with me and of course I couldn't do that."

"No." Frank laughed. "Of course you couldn't."

The young pilot congratulated the Hardys on the fine job they had done in uncovering Peterson's scheme against Mr. Allen. The boys felt gratified, but longed to solve another mystery. It was to come as they worked to find out the riddle of a story about *What Happened at Midnight.*

Mr. Allen heartily echoed Clint Hill's praise. "And since you Hardy boys are the best sleuths in the business," Mr. Allen added, "you've probably figured out that you are now looking at Stanwide's permanent chief pilot! That is," he added, with a grin in Clint's direction, "if our ghost gets around to shaving off those whiskers!"

Order Form
New revised editions of
THE BOBBSEY TWINS®

In *hardcover* at your local bookseller OR
simply mail in this handy order coupon and start your collection today!

Mail order form to: PUTNAM PUBLISHING GROUP/Mail Order Department
390 Murray Hill Parkway, East Rutherford, NJ 07073

ORDERED BY

Name _____

Address _____

City & State _____ Zip Code _____

Please send me the following Bobbsey Twins titles I've checked below.
All Books Priced @ $4.95

AVOID DELAYS   Please Print Order Form Clearly

☐ 1. Of Lakeport   448-09071-6   ☐ 8. Big Adventure at Home   448-09134-8
☐ 2. Adventure in the Country 448-09072-4   ☐ 10. On Blueberry Island   448-40110-X
☐ 3. Secret at the Seashore   448-09073-2   ☐ 11. Mystery on the
☐ 4. Mystery at School   448-09074-0   Deep Blue Sea   448-40113-4
☐ 5. At Snow Lodge   448-09098-8   ☐ 12. Adventure in
☐ 6. On a Houseboat   448-09099-6   Washington   448-40111-8
☐ 7. Mystery at Meadowbrook 448-09100-3   ☐ 13. Visit to the Great West   448-40112-6

Own the original exciting
BOBBSEY TWINS® ADVENTURE STORIES
still available:

☐ 13. Visit to the Great West   448-08013-3
☐ 14. And the Cedar Camp Mystery   448-08014-1

ALL ORDERS MUST BE PREPAID

_____ Payment Enclosed

_____ Visa

_____ Mastercard-Interbank #

Card # _____

Expiration Date _____

Signature _____
(Minimum Credit Card order of $10.00)

Postage and Handling Charges as follows

$2.00 for one book

$ .50 for each additional book thereafter

(Maximum charge of $4.95)

Merchandise total   _____

Shipping and Handling   _____

Applicable Sales Tax   _____

Total Amount
(U.S. currency only)   [   ]

The Bobbsey Twins series is a trademark of Simon & Schuster, Inc.,
and is registered in the United States Patent and Trademark Office.

Please allow 4 to 6 weeks for delivery.

Order Form
Own the original 58 action-packed
HARDY BOYS MYSTERY STORIES®

In *hardcover* at your local bookseller OR
simply mail in this handy order coupon and start your collection today!

Mail order form to   PUTNAM PUBLISHING GROUP/Mail Order Department
390 Murray Hill Parkway, East Rutherford, NJ 07073

ORDERED BY
Name _____

Address _____

City & State _____ Zip Code _____

Please send me the following Hardy Boys titles I've checked below
All Books Priced @ $4.95.

AVOID DELAYS   Please Print Order Form Clearly

☐	1	Tower Treasure	448-08901-7	☐ 30	Wailing Siren Mystery	448-08930-0
☐	2	House on the Cliff	448-08902-5	☐ 31	Secret of Wildcat Swamp	448-08931-9
☐	3	Secret of the Old Mill	448-08903-3	☐ 32	Crisscross Shadow	448-08932-7
☐	4	Missing Chums	448-08904-1	☐ 33	The Yellow Feather Mystery	448-08933-5
☐	5	Hunting for Hidden Gold	448-08905-X	☐ 34	The Hooded Hawk Mystery	448-08934-3
☐	6	Shore Road Mystery	448-08906-8	☐ 35	The Clue in the Embers	448-08935-1
☐	7	Secret of the Caves	448-08907-6	☐ 36	The Secret of Pirates' Hill	448-08936-X
☐	8	Mystery of Cabin Island	448-08908-4	☐ 37	Ghost at Skeleton Rock	448-08937-8
☐	9	Great Airport Mystery	448-08909-2	☐ 38	Mystery at Devil's Paw	448-08938-6
☐	10	What Happened at Midnight	448-08910-6	☐ 39	Mystery of the Chinese Junk	448-08939-4
☐	11	While the Clock Ticked	448-08911-4	☐ 40	Mystery of the Desert Giant	448-08940-8
☐	12	Footprints Under the Window	448-08912-2	☐ 41	Clue of the Screeching Owl	448-08941-6
☐	13	Mark on the Door	448-08913-0	☐ 42	Viking Symbol Mystery	448-08942-4
☐	14	Hidden Harbor Mystery	448-08914-9	☐ 43	Mystery of the Aztec Warrior	448-08943-2
☐	15	Sinister Sign Post	448-08915-7	☐ 44	The Haunted Fort	448-08944-0
☐	16	A Figure in Hiding	448-08916-5	☐ 45	Mystery of the Spiral Bridge	448-08945-9
☐	17	Secret Warning	448-08917-3	☐ 46	Secret Agent on Flight 101	448-08946-7
☐	18	Twisted Claw	448-08918-1	☐ 47	Mystery of the Whale Tattoo	448-08947-5
☐	19	Disappearing Floor	448-08919-X	☐ 48	The Arctic Patrol Mystery	448-08948-3
☐	20	Mystery of the Flying Express	448-08920-3	☐ 49	The Bombay Boomerang	448-08949-1
☐	21	The Clue of the Broken Blade	448-08921-1	☐ 50	Danger on Vampire Trail	448-08950-5
☐	22	The Flickering Torch Mystery	448-08922-X	☐ 51	The Masked Monkey	448-08951-3
☐	23	Melted Coins	448-08923-8	☐ 52	The Shattered Helmet	448-08952-1
☐	24	Short-Wave Mystery	448-08924-6	☐ 53	The Clue of the Hissing Serpent	448-08953-X
☐	25	Secret Panel	448-08925-4	☐ 54	The Mysterious Caravan	448-08954-8
☐	26	The Phantom Freighter	448-08926-2	☐ 55	The Witchmaster's Key	448-08955-6
☐	27	Secret of Skull Mountain	448-08927-0	☐ 56	The Jungle Pyramid	448-08956-4
☐	28	The Sign of the Crooked Arrow	448-08928-9	☐ 57	The Firebird Rocket	448-08957-2
☐	29	The Secret of the Lost Tunnel	448-08929-7	☐ 58	The Sting of the Scorpion	448-08958-0

Also Available The Hardy Boys Detective Handbook 448-01990-6

ALL ORDERS MUST BE PREPAID

_____ Payment Enclosed

_____ Visa

_____ Mastercard-Interbank #

Card # _____

Expiration Date_____

Signature_____
(Minimum Credit Card order of $10.00)

Postage and Handling Charges as follows

$2.00 for one book

$ .50 for each additional book thereafter

(Maximum charge of $4.95)

Merchandise total   _____

Shipping and Handling   _____

Applicable Sales Tax   _____

Total Amount   [   ]
(U.S. currency only)

Nancy Drew® and The Hardy Boys® are trademarks of Simon & Schuster, Inc.,
and are registered in the United States Patent and Trademark Office.

Please allow 4 to 6 weeks for delivery

DETACH ALONG DOTTED LINE AND MAIL IN ENVELOPE WITH PAYMENT

Order Form

Own the original 56 thrilling
NANCY DREW MYSTERY STORIES®

In *hardcover* at your local bookseller OR
simply mail in this handy order coupon and start your collection today!

Mail order form to   PUTNAM PUBLISHING GROUP/Mail Order Department
390 Murray Hill Parkway. East Rutherford. NJ 07073

ORDERED BY
Name _____

Address _____

City & State _____ Zip Code _____

Please send me the following Nancy Drew titles I've checked below
All Books Priced @ $4.95.

AVOID DELAYS   Please Print Order Form Clearly

☐	1	Secret of the Old Clock	448-09501-7	☐ 29	Mystery at the Ski Jump	448-09529-7
☐	2	Hidden Staircase	448-09502-5	☐ 30	Clue of the Velvet Mask	448-09530-0
☐	3	Bungalow Mystery	448-09503-3	☐ 31	Ringmaster's Secret	448-09531-9
☐	4	Mystery at Lilac Inn	448-09504-1	☐ 32	Scarlet Slipper Mystery	448-09532-7
☐	5	Secret of Shadow Ranch	448-09505-X	☐ 33	Witch Tree Symbol	448-09533-5
☐	6	Secret of Red Gate Farm	448-09506-8	☐ 34	Hidden Window Mystery	448-09534-3
☐	7	Clue in the Diary	448-09507-6	☐ 35	Haunted Showboat	448-09535-1
☐	8	Nancy's Mysterious Letter	448-09508-4	☐ 36	Secret of the Golden Pavilion	448-09536-X
☐	9	The Sign of the Twisted Candles	448-09509-2	☐ 37	Clue in the Old Stagecoach	448-09537-8
☐	10	Password to Larkspur Lane	448-09510-6	☐ 38	Mystery of the Fire Dragon	448-09538-6
☐	11	Clue of the Broken Locket	448-09511-4	☐ 39	Clue of the Dancing Puppet	448-09539-4
☐	12	The Message in the Hollow Oak	448-09512-2	☐ 40	Moonstone Castle Mystery	448-09540-8
☐	13	Mystery of the Ivory Charm	448-09513-0	☐ 41	Clue of the Whistling Bagpipes	448-09541-6
☐	14	The Whispering Statue	448-09514-9	☐ 42	Phantom of Pine Hill	448-09542-4
☐	15	Haunted Bridge	448-09515-7	☐ 43	Mystery of the 99 Steps	448-09543-2
☐	16	Clue of the Tapping Heels	448-09516-5	☐ 44	Clue in the Crossword Cipher	448-09544-0
☐	17	Mystery of the Brass-Bound Trunk	448-09517-3	☐ 45	Spider Sapphire Mystery	448-09545-9
☐	18	Mystery at Moss-Covered Mansion	448-09518-1	☐ 46	The Invisible Intruder	448-09546-7
☐	19	Quest of the Missing Map	448-09519-X	☐ 47	The Mysterious Mannequin	448-09547-5
☐	20	Clue in the Jewel Box	448-09520-3	☐ 48	The Crooked Banister	448-09548-3
☐	21	The Secret in the Old Attic	448-09521-1	☐ 49	The Secret of Mirror Bay	448-09549-1
☐	22	Clue in the Crumbling Wall	448-09522-X	☐ 50	The Double Jinx Mystery	448-09550-5
☐	23	Mystery of the Tolling Bell	448-09523-8	☐ 51	Mystery of the Glowing Eye	448-09551-3
☐	24	Clue in the Old Album	448-09524-6	☐ 52	The Secret of the Forgotten City	448-09552-1
☐	25	Ghost of Blackwood Hall	448-09525-4	☐ 53	The Sky Phantom	448-09553-X
☐	26	Clue of the Leaning Chimney	448-09526-2	☐ 54	The Strange Message in the Parchment	448-09554-8
☐	27	Secret of the Wooden Lady	448-09527-0	☐ 55	Mystery of Crocodile Island	448-09555-6
☐	28	The Clue of the Black Keys	448-09528-9	☐ 56	The Thirteenth Pearl	448-09556-4

ALL ORDERS MUST BE PREPAID

Postage and Handling Charges as follows

_____ Payment Enclosed

$2.00 for one book

_____ Visa

$ .50 for each additional book thereafter

_____ Mastercard-Interbank #

(Maximum charge of $4.95)

Card # _____

Merchandise total _____

Shipping and Handling _____

Expiration Date_____

Applicable Sales Tax _____

Signature_____
(Minimum Credit Card order of $10.00)

Total Amount
(U.S. currency only)   [_____]

Nancy Drew™ and The Hardy Boys® are trademarks of Simon & Schuster, Inc.,
and are registered in the United States Patent and Trademark Office

Please allow 4 to 6 weeks for delivery

DETACH ALONG DOTTED LINE AND MAIL IN ENVELOPE WITH PAYMENT